choosing FOREVER

MIA KAYLA

Cover Designer:
Sommer Stein, Perfect Pair Creative

Cover Photography:
© 2017 Scott Hoover

Interior Design & Formatting:
Christine Borgford, Type A Formatting

Developmental Editor:
Megan Hand

Copy Editor:
Jovana Shirley, Unforeseen Editing

Proofreader:
Shawna Gavas, Behind the Writer

choosing
FOREVER

To my writer and reader and blogger friends . . .

Thank you for believing in me, lifting me up, sending me sweet PMs and continuing to read my books. I've met some great people in this book world and am forever grateful..

chapter ONE

"HAWKE." I KISSED HIS FACE to wake him. "Are you okay?"

No response.

All my muscles tensed. Everything in my body screamed to push the panic button, but I kept steady.

I lifted his head, but it dropped against the pillow.

Then, pure hysteria slapped me in the face. My heartbeat raced. Full-body tremors overtook me.

My hands shook him as I said his name, slowly at first, but then my voice heightened to a crazed tone. "Hawke!"

My head dropped to his chest.

Hearing nothing.

But cold, dead silence.

Something was wrong. Tears coursed down my face as I pushed at his shoulders, the bed shaking from my movements. For a brief moment, I flashed back to my mother's room, trying to get her to wake up but it wasn't working. Wasn't working because she was already dead.

Tilton busted into our bedroom, like a man charging into a heist.

My vision was blurry from my tears. My breathing was raging from my panic. My hearing was muffled from my screams.

His eyes assessed the situation in two seconds before he stormed out of the room.

Hysteria inside me climbed to an uncontrollable state. "Hawke!" I cried, trying to revive him.

Suddenly, multiple people rushed into the area at once.

I heard someone say, "Call Alan." Like Alan was God or something.

My eyes, my focus, my hands were all on Hawke.

I pounded into his flesh, words slurring through my dread. I told him not to leave. I told him I needed him. I told him I was here for him. But I couldn't shake this fear, this horror I felt in my gut.

Strong arms wrapped around my waist. Familiar arms. But my hands were outstretched, reaching for my boyfriend. A woman, Alan, and another tall male I didn't recognize now surrounded Hawke as I was being pulled away. Away from my man. The tall male had medical gloves, but he wasn't in scrubs. They propped Hawke up against the headboard, but he was still unresponsive. In the next second, the taller male took out a long syringe.

I screamed for them to stop because I didn't know what was going on. I kicked and yelled and fought the arms that were slowly taking me from the room. Before the door shut, I saw the tall male in jeans and a button-down shoot the syringe into Hawke's thigh.

Soft, muffled words were uttered above my head, "He'll be okay." The phrase was spoken over and over.

Two other bodyguards I recognized were pushing people out the door.

And then clarity hit me through all the fog.

This was the cleanup crew.

"Call Alan," someone had said.

He was the head janitor, cleaning up the mess.

The bouncers were clearing out the party.

The medical team surrounded Hawke's body.

And that syringe.

They were trying to save his life.

Tilton ushered me down the hall to another suite. The water works would not stop and no sounds left my mouth. I felt like one of those crying baby dolls you fed water to, face devoid of emotion but tears streaming down the cheeks.

By this time, I was hiccuping, and all Tilton could do was stand beside me, witnessing my breakdown.

Who knew how much time had passed, but when I peered up, Alan walked into the suite, smiling, as though nothing had happened. I wanted to ask if Hawke was okay. I wanted to beg him to let me see him, but I didn't want to talk to Alan directly. Because I was disgusted. I couldn't believe someone who was supposed to keep them together and safe would allow this.

Alan ran one hand through his curly dark hair, strolled to the bar, and poured some copper-colored liquor into a glass. "Drink?" he asked me.

All I could do was glare at him, inhaling and exhaling to calm myself. I had no words for him. None.

"He's okay," he said, shrugging, as if everything was fine.

I still hated him, but the relief that came over me was overpowering. I cowered into myself, dropping my head into my hands. My whole body visibly trembled with relief.

I'd had an inkling that Hawke was okay, but now that I was sure, all my emotions poured out in tears for Alan and Tilton to witness. The situation reminded me of my mother. The memories of her and the pain I'd felt burned brightly in my brain. I was reliving the past—only, this time, my loved one was okay. He was alive.

"Sam."

I shook my head. I didn't want to hear it. I didn't want to know what Alan had to say.

"You're going home, Sam."

I lifted my head and sucked in a breath when Alan threw a stack of hundreds onto the bed. It was held together by a single rubber band.

"Just don't make contact. Don't talk to the press, and we're good." He gulped back his drink, his eyes studying me.

I blinked a couple of times before finding the ability to speak.

"Are you paying me off?" I hiccuped. "For what?"

"To keep your mouth shut and leave him alone." He turned away from me and poured some powdered substance into his glass.

What is wrong with the people here?

How could they throw people away like trash when it didn't suit them anymore?

Their money and power had no limits.

The drugs. The partying. The lies.

I guessed he would allow the band to live this sort of lifestyle as long as their talents fed his pockets.

"Sam, Sam, Sam," he said, his tone low and condescending, "do you think this is the first time I've been down this road with Hawke?"

His words confirmed my doubts, and I bit my tongue to prevent any emotions from showing on my face. If he was bluffing, I wanted to keep my best poker face on.

"He's like this every weekend." He let out a cynical laugh that had invisible spiders biting every inch of my skin with venom so strong, it kept me from moving. "Except when you're around," he muttered under his breath.

"You're lying." My voice was steady, my eyes firmly on his, assessing his reaction.

He shook his head and tipped his chin toward Tilton behind me. "These chicks, they always think they're special, don't they? One of a kind, that our boys will change their ways for them. If you think you're the only one, honey, I hate to break it to you"—he let out a bitter laugh—"but you're not."

He tipped back his drink, finished it off, and then met my stare. "But there is something about you. Yes, I'll admit that. Hawke has never been as hung up on anyone as he's been with you. But, still, it hasn't stopped him from screwing anything with two legs and big tits."

I stood, my fists clenched at my sides, all self-control gone.

"You're a liar!" I shouted. "You're probably their dealer, aren't you? If they're so high on whatever you gave them, then they'll do as you say."

He chuckled darkly. "You'd like to believe that, wouldn't you? That I'm their master, and they're my puppets? So that when he's inside another woman, it's my fault, not his? Dumb girls." He nodded at Tilton. "Get her out of here. First flight back to wherever she's from."

Then, he stalked out of the room, leaving me an emotional, manic mess.

My hands shook and all I felt was numbness from the tips of my fingers to the middle of my chest. My breathing came in big, broken puffs. I needed a bag to hyperventilate into.

Alan was lying; he had to be.

"Miss Clarke."

When I glanced at Tilton, he held the door open, waiting for me to make my exit. From the slight movement of his mouth, I knew he felt sorry for me. But he didn't have to because, for the first time since I had been thrown into this love affair, I felt sorry for myself.

Alan's words had been like a sledgehammer to my heart, but I had made the choice to come here. I had chosen to be Hawke's girlfriend when I knew what his life was like. I knew how many girls threw themselves at him every day.

Pushing down the pain, I followed Tilton out and took the walk of shame down to the lobby. I'd left my backpack in Hawke's room, the money on the bed, and my heart in Seattle as I headed back home because I no longer cared.

I WALKED THROUGH MY APARTMENT door in a daze, my cheeks still stained with dry tears. The morning sun was shining through our curtains, indicating the beginning of a new day, and my heart constricted. Because the beginning of one day meant the end of another.

My lips quivered, and my mind flew to the night before, seeing Hawke's unresponsive body lying on the silky satin beneath him. Fresh tears rolled down my cheeks as I trudged to my best friend's room.

When I opened the door, Chloe lifted her head from her pillow.

One look at my face had her jumping up and wrapping her arms around me. "Oh, Sam. What happened?"

Sobs shook my shoulders as I collapsed into her arms. Being in her arms brought me back to years ago. Chloe had held me during my darkest moments when my mother had fallen into a deep depression, and I couldn't deal. Chloe had held me then, and she was holding me now.

She pulled me down to the edge of the bed and then went to grab some tissues on her desk by the window as I cowered into myself.

"What happened?" she asked, her face filled with concern. "What did he do?"

I cupped my hand to my mouth, not knowing where I should begin. Talking about it would make it more real. The reality of my situation was that my relationship with Hawke had been a made-up lie, but more than that was his condition.

I reached into my back pocket and pulled out his phone.

"What's going on, Sam?"

I shook my head and brought the phone to my ear. The call went to an automated voice mail, and dread washed over me. I knew he was most likely unconscious or recovering, but the insane part of me just wanted to hear his voice for myself to know that he was okay.

"What did the asshole do now?" she asked, her tone inflamed with anger, her expression clouded with rage.

I hung up and called again. The ringing in my ear drowned out my friend's voice.

After she grabbed the phone and threw it on the bed, she framed my shoulders. "What's wrong?"

Looking into her concerned hazel eyes broke the silence within me. "I just need to know that he's okay. They said he's okay, but I need to hear him for myself." My breathing slowed as I recalled the male shooting a syringe into Hawke's body. "I just need to know. He needs to be okay."

"Why wouldn't he be?" She shook my shoulders. "Sam! Why wouldn't he be?"

My hands flew to my ravaged heart as I tried to take deep breaths through my nose to calm down.

"Sam! Look at me!" Her eyes blazed, her tone bristling with building hysteria.

"Because he died. It felt like he did."

I fell to my knees, and Chloe dropped beside me, taking both of my hands into hers.

"Hawke isn't dead, Sam. He can't be."

"He was dying, Chloe. He was unresponsive." I hiccupped and closed my eyes to drown out the havoc in my thoughts.

"Why?" she whispered.

"He was on something. I don't know what."

I swiped at my wet eyes and reached for the phone again, but Chloe blocked me.

"No, you don't." Fierce determination was in her tone. "He was high on something he had taken. It was his choice, and as mean as it sounds, it's not your problem."

I threw both hands in the air. "How can you say that?"

"Because he probably does this every weekend!" Her eyes dimmed like dark and angry thunderclouds.

"Then, I have to help him." The need to be there, to stop history from repeating itself, was eating at my core.

"Stop right there," Chloe ordered, squeezing my hand. "You

think this is a repeat of the past, and it's not." Chloe's voice softened as she ducked and leaned in closer. "You couldn't save your mom because she didn't want to be saved. Hawke is not suicidal, Sam. Maybe he was dealt some bad cards with his mother, but it's his choice how he handles it, not yours."

"Chloe," I begged, trying to reach around her for the phone.

She shook her head, her face resolute. "No, I'm not letting you do this to yourself all over again. I love you too much."

She chucked the phone toward the other end of the room. The thud against her floor resonated in my ears.

She tugged my hand, bringing me into one of her signature warm embraces. "He's going to be okay, but what matters most is that you're okay. And, as your best friend, I'm going to personally make sure that happens."

I fell into her arms, exhausted, as she uttered over and over that everything would be okay.

I didn't go after my phone again. I simply let her consoling tone calm me.

But I couldn't help but wonder, *Will it all be okay?*

chapter TWO

EVERY HOUR, EVERY MINUTE, EVERY second dragged on like a painful surgery. Except, this time, there was nothing that could fix my broken heart.

A week later, I watched Hawke on my flat screen television. He was sitting on a chair, surrounded by his band members, laughing and answering the interviewer's questions, as though everything were right with the world. His face was flushed with color, opposite to the man I'd left unresponsive in his bed in Seattle. The only indication that anything was wrong was the dullness in his green eyes that were normally full of life.

Knowing he was alive and breathing helped my mind, but it didn't curb the pain in the center of my chest. Pain from our break-up and pain from my past.

Chloe had confiscated my secret phone so that, if Hawke called, I wouldn't know. She'd reiterated that I had to stop this crazy obsession I had with him. Though I cared for him, a part of me knew she was right.

Seeing the booze and the hard-core drugs had told me he was playing with a whole different crowd that I had no business dealing with. At first, I had been with him for the adventure, to live out of my comfort zone. To embrace my life in my twenties because I'd grown up quickly after taking care of my mother for so long. But that life in the fast lane was just not me.

I was heartbroken but not dumb. I wasn't so naive as to believe that a stable life of marriage and children would happen with him.

I stretched my arms over my head as the sun seeped in through Chloe's curtains. I'd been sleeping in her room these past couple of nights because the nightmares had returned. The ones where I was back in Carbarny, shaking my mom's lifeless body.

I had called off work these last few days because I was sick. Bundled up under the covers, tissues in my hand, and snot in my nose. I was at home, sick from a broken heart and from memories that continued to haunt me. No amount of medicine or doctors could fix that, only time. I knew this. I'd been down this road before.

"I have to get to work and meet some clients. Are you going to be okay?" Chloe asked before lifting the covers over my head. "I called in food-forcements." Her word for *reinforcements*.

She opened her door but not before glancing back and saying, "Brush your teeth, okay? It's been a while." She was dressed in a fitted pinstriped skirt suit and ruffle-collared blouse—what I'd call business cute and casual. "Love you. I'll be in the living room."

When she exited the room, I blew out a long breath and stared blankly at the ceiling above me. I needed to move on with my life, and it needed to start now.

That was why Chloe wasn't just my best friend, but she was also my soul friend, the person who I knew would be in my life until we were old and gray and in wheelchairs.

I forced myself to stand, and I strolled into her bathroom. As I brushed my teeth, I stared at my sore red eyes in the mirror. I would be a perfect fit for a Visine commercial right about now.

After pulling my hair into a bun, I staggered out into the living room and stopped mid step. Josh was standing there, holding a Coozie's pizza box.

I hadn't seen him since I'd left, but he'd called me numerous times. As soon as his warm eyes met mine, I realized I'd missed him badly.

"Hey." I blinked back tears and waved a hand his way.

His eyes drifted from me to Chloe before he dropped the pizza box on the coffee table.

He didn't know.

Chloe hadn't told him.

He slowly walked toward me, looking me over to see if any part of me was hurt. Too bad I hurt from the inside out.

"Everything okay?"

The concern in his eyes nearly broke me, but I maintained my composure.

"Yes."

Chloe huffed behind him. "It's called Asshole Syndrome. Don't catch it. The only cure is a good kick in the balls."

After seeing Hawke on TV, any compassion from Chloe for his state had flown out the window.

Chloe blew me a kiss before slipping on her suit jacket. "Take care of my girl, okay?"

Words were exchanged between Josh and Chloe, but I just plopped on the couch and stared blankly at the TV.

I had known it wouldn't work out with me and Hawke, so I didn't understand why I was so disappointed. I blew out a breath.

When the door shut, I felt the couch cushion dip beside me. I blew out small puffs of air to prevent myself from crying again. I didn't want to fall apart in front of Josh. You'd think I was all cried out. I guessed not.

But then I felt Josh's warmth around me. He said nothing as his arms picked me up and set me on his lap. With his fingertips, he touched my cheek and then swiped the wetness from under my eyes.

One touch.

One breath.

One look.

That was all it took to make me collapse, holding my stomach to keep myself together.

This is part of the process, I told myself. *Time heals all. And all will eventually be forgotten.*

Gently, he pulled my arms apart and wrapped them around his waist, and I relented, falling into the comfort of his arms. He brushed a tender kiss across my forehead, and I buried my face in the corded muscles of his chest.

"The worst thing in the world," he began, "is hearing you cry." He tucked me under his chin and brought me closer. "Because you don't do it often. And here I thought, you had superhuman powers with the inability to shed a tear."

My hands gripped his sides as I sobbed softly. In his gentle embrace, all self-control flew out the window. I hadn't realized how much I needed this physical contact.

"Shh." He squeezed me against him, and his breath hitched. "Tormented puppies, wailing babies . . . I think I could handle all of that. What I can't handle is seeing you like this. Whatever it is, I'm sure it will be okay."

"We're done," I croaked out.

I felt the expansion of his chest against my cheek. After a few minutes, I lifted my head and stared into his eyes. "Say it," I whispered. "Tell me you told me so. Tell me you're happy this happened. Say something."

Part of me expected him to be happy even if silently, but as his eyebrows knit together, only concern clouded his vision.

With his fingertips, he tipped up my chin. "As selfish as this might sound, I wanted this to happen. Because I knew he never deserved you." He ran his thumb under one of my tear-filled eyes. "But, after seeing you like this . . . I can't want anything that's hurt you this much."

I swiped my eyes against the sleeve of my shirt.

"Stop crying, Princess." He smirked. "I need that sarcastic, fun-loving girl back, and I'll bring her back however I can." He narrowed his eyes, contemplating. "What do you want me to do? Call him? Tell him he's made a big mistake? Because I guarantee you, he already knows that."

Alan's words rang loudly in my ears. The lies. Nothing but lies.

"No, I don't want that. It's just . . ." My gaze dropped to my lap. "I don't know what I was expecting, and maybe that's where my downfall was . . . I expected more." With my sleeve, I swiped under my nose. "He was the one who wanted to do this . . . be in a relationship. But you can't base a relationship on lies."

He sucked in his bottom lip, his eyes telling me they wanted more intel, but I was out of energy. I wanted to tell him everything. About Hawke, about the drugs, about him lying motionless, as if he were dead. But not now. I couldn't relive what had happened.

I averted my gaze as fresh tears formed. "I'll be okay. I'll make myself okay."

"Of course you'll be okay. Pfft. Remember?" A small smile touched his lips. "You've got superhuman powers. And I also have a theory," Josh said. "I don't think you're even crying about this breakup."

I wrinkled my nose. "Oh, yeah?"

"Yeah." He angled closer, our noses almost touching. "The real reason you're crying is because it's that time of the month, and you ladies get really emotional during this time." His face was devoid of any emotion, his eyes serious.

When I pinched his side, he flinched and held his arm, feigning pain. "See? Superhuman powers."

"You're so failing at trying to make this better," I said with a watery laugh.

"Why are you smiling then?" He grinned.

"I'm not." I tried to stop the smile that curved my mouth, but with Josh, it was hard to do that.

"It's an almost smile. I'll take it." After I scooted off his lap, he stood and extended a hand. "Let's go. I also know, during that time of the month, you gals get really, really hungry. We need to bust open that Coozie's box."

I stared at his outstretched hand, wondering how I'd get through the next few days.

"I'm serious," he insisted. "I grew up with two women in my household, and during those times, my father and I would stay away."

When I didn't move, he bent down and said, "Exhale, Sam. One breath at a time."

I stared up into his chocolate-brown eyes and released one big breath.

Exhale.

After a beat, I stood and placed my hand in his. That familiar warmth, the one that only Josh could give me, spread up my arm. "Are you the master of all women now?"

One side of his mouth ticked up. "Pretty much. I plan to write a book. Kind of like *Men Are from Mars, Women Are from Venus*, but from my perspective."

One breath.

Air filled my lungs, and I straightened, digging up the deep-rooted strength I had within me.

"I want to read this book."

Another breath.

He took my arm and linked it through his. "Best seller, I'm telling ya." He winked, picked up the pizza box from the coffee table and led us into the kitchen.

As I followed him, a tiny flicker of hope bloomed in my chest, for a life where Hawke was well and where I'd be okay, too.

chapter THREE

I PUSHED THE CART THROUGH the grocery store, staring blankly at the rows and rows of cereal. Cheerios, Cap'n Crunch, Lucky Charms. I'd been wandering aimlessly for a while. For some reason, I'd forgotten what I had to pick up.

Room service in Paris.

There were times when I thought I was okay and times when everything that had happened between Hawke and me would run through my head, playing back like a movie.

It had been a few weeks, but if he had tried to call me, I didn't know. One night, when I'd turned weak, I'd tried to search Chloe's room for my phone. I'd found it, but she had taken the battery out. And maybe, if she hadn't done that, I would've checked for messages. I avoided any news or media outlet where I might catch a glimpse of him. The radio, the Internet, and definitely the TV.

The days when I worked would go faster than when I was alone at home. But, when I was at home, I would bake like I was going to starve tomorrow. Because that was what I did when I was upset. I would bake for an army of men and eat it by my lonesome.

The only light in my long days was Josh. He'd help me bake. We'd watch movies, like we always did, and when he was in school or working, it was like he was still with me because he'd leave me random notes in the weirdest places.

In my fridge: *WTF (Where's the food?)*

In my jar of sugar: *Good things come to those who bake.*

In my coat pocket: *Where there is a whisk, there is a way!*

In my underwear drawer: *It doesn't matter if you win or lose; it's how you bake the cake.*

It was as if Josh had this power to determine the exact time I would be thinking of Hawke because I'd find these notes strategically placed in spots when I was in my lowest moments. The notes would make me smile and lift my mood, and I hoped for more.

As I stared at a box of Quaker Oatmeal Squares, my phone rang in my back pocket, and I picked it up.

"Princess, where are you?"

Automatically, the corners of my mouth lifted, and the Hawke fog dimmed around me. "At the grocery store, getting food for movie night. I think I've officially gained ten pounds from everything we've baked."

He laughed. "So, do we still have the five dozen cookies from yesterday?"

"Josh, really, do you think I could have eaten all of that by myself?" I reached for the shelf and decided on a box of Lucky Charms. "Okay, fine. There are probably four dozen cookies left."

"Do you want to do something different today?"

I glanced down at my sweats and T-shirt—my grumpy post-breakup wear. *Not really.* "Sure!" I said with forced gusto.

"Get ready, and pack the cookies. I'll pick you up at your place."

And that was exactly what I did.

I rushed home and changed into a bright yellow silk shirt, dark-washed skinny jeans, and my thick peacoat. Then, I slipped into my favorite Converse, packed the cookies in Tupperware, and waited for Josh on the couch while reality TV played in the background.

After he rang my doorbell, I rushed outside to meet him. I didn't ask where we were going as we hopped in the back of a cab. I didn't ask what we were doing with four-dozen cookies. I didn't care where we went as long as it was anywhere but home, as long as it was somewhere I could keep my mind busy, and I knew Josh could do that.

When the cab stopped in front of a brown building, I pushed my face against the window, taking in my surroundings. In copper letters on a silver plaque against the brown brick read, *Department of Child and Family Services.*

"Where are we?" I asked, looking up at Josh.

"It's where I volunteer sometimes and where I want to end up working eventually once I'm finished with law school." His eyes lit with an inner glow, and a slight smile touched his face as he stared at the building in front of us.

I knew Josh worked for a hotshot adoption lawyer in the heart of downtown Chicago. The guy's office was on the fifty-sixth floor of a modern skyscraper. I'd assumed that was where Josh wanted to end up, but by the way his eyes brightened, I realized I was wrong.

"You want to work here?" I asked.

"Yeah, once I'm done."

As we walked into the building that seemed to be over one hundred years old, I heard laughter, followed by an array of little kids running about in the foyer. They were a hodgepodge of different ethnicities and ages.

I was going to ask Josh what was going on when a little girl, no more than four, flew into his arms.

"Joshy!"

Joshy?

Her dark brown ringlets danced as she looked at Josh through her light-hazel eyes, as though he were Santa Claus bringing her presents. "Where did you go, Joshy? I thought you left me, too."

His eyes broke a little, and so did my heart. "I'm sorry, Ana. I've been busy, but you know I'd never leave you."

"Better not. You my *boyfend*. You said so," she said with such sass that I laughed.

He laughed, too. "Only you, Anabelle. Only you."

My insides melted into a puddle of goo. Swoon. Ovary explosion.

He tipped his head in my direction and held Anabelle against his hip. "I brought a friend, and she brought cookies."

Miss Anabelle was not happy to see me. Her arms crossed over her chest, and she was sporting a very nasty stink eye. I smiled up at her, knowing full well she had every right to be mad at me since I was the reason *Joshy* had been so busy.

I opened the Tupperware, smiling bigger to win over this cute but tough child. "They're chocolate chip, and Joshy, your boyfriend, made them just for you."

We'd baked them together, but she didn't need to know that.

Josh gently placed her on the ground. Ana seemed a little hesitant at first as she approached me, but when I angled the Tupperware in her direction, she dipped her cute, skinny fingers inside and reached for a cookie.

"Thank you," she said with a begrudging frown. It was as if it had taken all her energy to utter those two words.

"Josh!"

I peered up to see a tall woman in a cream dress suit rushing toward us. Her dark bob swished against her cheeks. "Oh my goodness, we've missed you." She pulled him in for a half-hug. "I'm so glad you came. You just missed the mayor."

A clown with balloons passed in front of us, followed by another clown with two puppies dressed in frill.

Ana's eyes brightened. "Joshy, Clappy the Clown is here! See ya later." She waved her cookie in the air and bounced along with the other children heading toward Clappy.

"Oh, that Ana," the woman said, releasing Josh. The cream-colored suit brought out her olive-toned skin. The woman seemed to be in her early fifties with a dust of white highlighting her dark hair. "And Jessica, Jennifer, and Clara. They've all been asking about their"—she put her fingers in air quotes—"'boyfriend.'"

Her smile exuded warmth, and I immediately liked her.

"I'm Shannon Barnes, Director here at Chicago's DCFS. You

must be Josh's girlfriend."

I shook her hand. "No, just a friend. I'm Samantha, but you can call me Sam."

"Well, Sam, just so you know, Josh is a player of sorts around here." Her smile widened, and she threw him a cursory glance. "Lots of girlfriends and all," she joked.

Josh gave a sheepish smile. "I'm sorry I haven't been around lately."

Shannon held up a hand. "No excuses necessary. I know you're busy. The kids just miss you; that's all. They miss your jokes and your coloring abilities." She tipped her head to the side.

I raised my eyebrows. "Coloring abilities? Josh, you've been holding out on me."

Josh's cheeks reddened, but in the next second, he threw up his hands and spread his fingers, wiggling them in my direction. "These hands can't bake, but boy, can they color. I've got mad artistic skills."

I barked out a laugh.

Shannon gestured behind him. "Let's take Sam on a tour. We have an indoor bouncy house today and face-painting. The kids are having a blast."

Her eyes lit up with excitement, and a big part of me believed she wanted to hop in the bouncy house herself.

I walked beside Josh, distributing cookies to his little friends. He had quite a few. And Shannon was not joking; the little girls loved him.

"So, once a quarter, we hold these events for the children," Shannon said, rubbing a little boy's head as he passed by. "A lot of them are still in foster care, looking for a permanent home."

I nodded, fascinated by everything in my vicinity. It was like Disney World. Cinderella skipped past me, holding hands with two girls who looked up at her with their childlike wonder. In the other corner of the room, Captain America, cape and all, was showing the boys some card tricks.

I trailed behind Shannon as she entered another area that was occupied by little girls in their fluffy princess dresses. Princess Elsa sat in the middle of the room, reading a book to the children all seated around her.

"The mayor comes in, and all these people here volunteer their services to show the children a good time. A lot of these children are in protective custody and have dealt with distress in their former home environment. We get children straight from the hospital sometimes." A frown formed heavy on her face, her stare becoming distant. "Some were plucked from their homes because of their living conditions. Roach-infested homes. Abuse. Sex offenders. These parents believe they still have a right to these innocent children just because they birthed them into the world."

She turned toward Josh and put a hand on his arm. "That's why your job is so important." She smiled up at him. "Fighting for their rights in that courtroom is no easy task. Protect the innocent, Joshy."

Josh placed his hand over Shannon's, his eyes firm. "I will. I need to graduate first and earn my cape. Then, it's Super Joshy to the rescue."

She laughed and proceeded farther down the hall to continue our tour. After a minute, we plopped down around a set of small tables. My butt barely fit in the chair, but I made it work.

"Josh!"

Two boys went to do a signature handshake, fist over fist and ending in a thumbs-up. They looked like they were around middle school age. One boy had a gap between his teeth, and the other boy's skin was badly scarred. One side of his face was wrinkled together, as though he was a burn victim.

My stomach clenched, and I tried to look into his eyes, not at his face.

"Is this your girlfriend, Josh?" Tilting his head, he took me in, and then he grinned. "I approve, bro. No wonder you haven't been around."

My smile widened at the bold, suave young man in front of me.

Josh laughed. "Chill, Rocky. She's just a friend." He pointed to the kid who exuded self-confidence. "And, good thing for you, she's single."

He nodded his head in slow motion. "Oh, I see. Well, Sam, if you want to come color with my sister and me, we are just at that other table." He angled his head toward said table.

I laughed and extended my hand. "I'd love to."

His eyes widened at my outstretched hand, his bravado gone. He blinked a little bit before stuttering out, "Uh . . . okay."

Josh pointed two fingers to his eyes and then pointed to Rocky. "I'm watching you, boy. This one here is special. You'd better treat her right. Let her have her choice of crayons."

Rocky saluted Josh and took my hand. Along with his friend, he escorted me to the table where his little sister was coloring. Her frame was tiny, and she must have been no more than four years old. Her red hair was in disarray, fanning out over her ears and onto her cheeks.

"This is Marty. Marty, Sam." He nodded at each of us.

When the little girl peered up at me, I noted a scar from her temple to her chin. I blew out a breath, choking back tears. I couldn't cry in front of these kids. They'd already been through so much. Today was a happy day, a celebration for them.

She looked down again, embarrassed. Unlike her older brother, she was very aware of her scar.

With my fingertips, I tipped up her chin. "Hey, beautiful. You have the prettiest hair I've ever seen. Do you know that Disney movie *Brave* with Princess Merida?"

She smiled, all teeth. "Yeah, it's my favorite movie in the whole wide world!"

"Has anyone told you that you look just like her?"

She nodded. "Yes. And Marty and Merida both start with an *M*."

"That's right!" I glanced over at the paper she was coloring. I sat down, barely fitting in the pink child-size chair and scooted in. "What are you coloring?"

"A puppy."

"Can I help?" I asked, picking up a brown crayon.

"It's a rainbow puppy."

"Well then, brown is the wrong color." I winked.

A sense of calm filled my insides as I laughed along with Marty, and we took turns coloring her puppy with an array of different shades. Soon, a crowd of kids formed around me, wanting me to help them turn their penguins, princesses, and hearts into rainbows. I guessed I had major coloring skills because, when Josh found me, my table was full. I even had a kid on my lap.

When I glanced at him, he was watching me with certain awe and other emotions I couldn't decipher.

"We're closing up shop now," he said softly.

"We are?" I glanced around and saw that the room had cleared out, and the only table still occupied was mine.

"Miss Sam, but you said it's my turn." A little girl with the greenest eyes stared up at me, sporting her puppy-dog pout.

I touched the tip of her nose. "Of course." I shrugged up at Josh. "One more?"

A dimple appeared on his cheek. "I'll just be outside, helping Shannon clean up."

After coloring the rest of the pages with my team, I hugged each of the kids twice, soaking in their joy. It was then that I realized my problems were nothing, my broken heart was nothing, compared to what some of these kids had endured.

I had to blink back tears again as I watched each of them. They all seemed hopeful, even after whatever they'd been through.

With a new perspective, I cleaned up the crayons and papers as the children dispersed into the foyer where some of the foster parents were picking them up. Shannon was talking with a group of three women while Josh had a broom in his hand, sweeping away.

"Wanna give me a hand, Cinderella?" he asked as I walked toward him.

"Sure. Do you have another one of those?"

In Josh's goofy way, he hopped on the broom, pretending to fly away on the stick like a witch. He returned with another broom in hand, the black bristles smacking me on the ass.

"Hey," I said, grabbing the end from his hand.

We tidied up, and once the kids were gone, music blasted in the background from the built-in speakers in the corners of the room. Clappy the Clown took off his wig and started shaking his stuff, garbage bag in hand. Meghan Trainor's "All About That Bass" echoed against the walls. Now that no kiddos were in sight, the adults were out to play.

My hips shook, my head nodded, my shoulders wiggled, all while I swept the floor. When "The Most Beautiful Girl in the World" by Prince played on the speakers, Josh took the edge of his broomstick, using it as a mic, and serenaded me. The volunteers gathered around us, waving their hands in the air, and I couldn't help but laugh. It didn't matter that he couldn't belt out a tune. He didn't look self-conscious at all. He just sang to me with all that he was and seemed to mean every word, as though it were his own personal concert.

Though my cheeks warmed, I placed one hand on my heart, playing the part.

It was a perfect moment.

But, when the next tune came on, Def Deception's "Undeniable," I stilled. Hearing Hawke's voice brought memories of him into my thoughts.

The smile on Josh's face disappeared, and for a moment, he looked panicked, his eyes searching the room, on a mission to turn off the radio.

I lifted a hand. "I'm okay," I insisted. Because I was.

The normal tension in the center of my chest had dimmed to a buzz, no longer an overwhelming ache.

Big people, little problems. Little kids, big problems. That was what today had taught me.

Josh was healing me in ways he probably didn't even realize.

Finally, when all the toys were put away and the brooms and mops were tucked in the closets, I went to the front where Josh was talking to Shannon.

When they saw me approach, she stepped forward and wrapped her arms around me in the warmest body-crushing hug. "Thanks for coming today, Sam." She pulled back and smiled. "I hope you come see us again."

"I will."

I definitely would. The whole day had lightened my spirits, and I had enjoyed being surrounded by the kids. I had needed this to help me decompress from work and life.

Josh and Shannon said their good-byes, and once Josh and I were out the door, the stars twinkled above us against the dark sky. We walked to the corner, hand in hand, and he stopped to raise his hand to hail a cab.

I stepped closer and wrapped my arms around his middle, pressing my head to his chest. "Thank you." Two words had my whole body relaxing into him.

His lips went to my hair. "For what?" he asked softly. "You helped me out today I should be thanking you."

I shook my head, my face rustling against his cotton T-shirt. "Just for being you."

He rubbed my back and his voice softened. "It's nothing."

I blew out a breath. He had no clue how much he did for me just by being my friend and being there for me.

It wasn't nothing.

It was everything.

chapter FOUR

INSIDE OUT WAS PLAYING ON my forty-five-inch TV in the living room. I loved this TV, remembering when Chloe and I had gotten it. We'd stayed up late and camped out in front of Walmart for last year's After Christmas sale.

I sighed in total peace. The sweet scent of brownies in the oven filtered through my nose, and my feet were in Josh's lap, the same place they'd been for the last few nights.

After Josh had cooked dinner for me and Chloe, she had left to go meet some coworkers at a bar. I had chosen Pixar, brownies, and Josh.

Josh glanced over at me. "If you could pick one Pixar character for me, who would it be?" His face was stone serious. No smile, no dimples.

"What?" I began to laugh.

"I'm serious." A dimple emerged on his cheek, but he clenched his jaw to prevent any laughter from spilling over. "Which one?"

I sucked in my bottom lip and scrunched my eyebrows, as though I were in deep concentration. I couldn't picture him as Sadness or Anger or Joy . . .

Not Woody or Buzz . . .

Then, it dawned on me.

I pointed a finger in his direction. "You are James P. Sullivan."

"Who?"

"Sulley from *Monsters Inc.*"

He still had a look of confusion on his face.

I sighed and spread my arms out wide. "The big blue guy with the purple spots?"

Clarity slowly entered his vision. "His name is James P. Sullivan?"

"Don't ask me how I remember these details. But, yes, you are so Sulley. You look all big and bad with your toned muscles, but—"

"You've noticed my muscles?" he cut me off as he quirked an eyebrow, amused.

The tips of my ears warmed, but I kept going. "But that's just your exterior. Sulley wants to do the right thing—for himself and for that little girl he tries to save, Boo. So, yeah"—I smiled—"you're Sulley."

He suggestively wiggled his eyebrows. "I'm still on the fact that you've noticed my muscles."

I tried to focus my stare on the screen again. "Please."

When Josh pushed up his sleeve and flexed, my attention to what was playing on the television was shot. The tendons on his forearms strained and I couldn't help but notice. He was built. Milk, working out, and playing ball had done his body good.

He gestured at his muscle. "You can touch it if you want to."

A smile formed on my face, but I kept my focus on the TV. "No, thanks. I'm good."

"Are you sure?" He leaned in closer, smirking. "Go ahead. Touch it. I don't mind." And then he kissed it for exaggerated effect.

I laughed even though a dizzying current flowed through my veins. "You're such a goofball, you know that?"

The house phone rang in the background, and I stood and walked to pick it up.

"What? They're nice, right?" He lifted both of his guns and made his muscles bounce.

What a sexy dork!

I shook my head, flipping around to face him. "I was talking about Sulley's muscles, not yours, silly."

"Those weren't your words," he contested. He narrowed one

eye, pretending to remember, though I was certain he hadn't forgotten. "I think you said something about my *toned* muscles."

Laughter erupted in my throat before I picked up the phone.

"Hello?" I said into the phone, still laughing.

"Hey, Sunshine." Hawke's voice was low and gruff. He sounded as though he were sick or maybe had been crying.

My hand shook as I gripped our house phone, my fingers visibly trembling. It wasn't like I had forgotten him. I hadn't. I'd done everything possible to avoid anything Hawke.

"You're hard to get ahold of."

My eyes fell shut. I should hang up the phone, but I couldn't. Hearing his voice only verified that he was well, alive. I knew he had made it through with that saving shot, but hearing his voice for myself was a different story.

"Sunshine?"

I couldn't speak. I pressed a hand to my heart, feeling a slew of emotions bubbling up inside my chest.

Seeing him motionless on his bed had brought up memories of my mother's death. A death that I'd spent years trying to heal from. A death that I blamed myself for. A death that I didn't want repeated.

I had a strong awareness of my heart beating loudly in my ears, like a river rushing against the shoreline.

"Princess?"

I turned to face Josh. When our eyes locked, he stood. But I placed one palm toward him and shook my head to stop him from coming closer.

"I saw her, Sunshine." Hawke's voice was barely above a whisper.

Immediately, heat formed behind my eyes, and I took the cordless phone into my room, giving Josh an apologetic expression before I shut the door.

"It's been years, and . . . I just saw her last week. She's dying.

She's dying for real," Hawke spoke in a soft, broken whisper.

My butt hit the edge of my mattress. My hands trembled against my comforter. I imagined his hurt, his pain, from the years of turmoil his mother had caused him, but in the end, it didn't matter. Because you only had one mother. And, now, his was dying.

Shallow breaths escaped him. "I called you after you left. You never picked up your phone."

I closed my eyes. So, he had called me. I wondered what Alan had told him, what Hawke knew about that night. If he remembered anything.

"I'm sorry about your mom," was all I could say.

Because, now that he was on the phone with me, now that I had a grip on my emotions, I realized I wasn't sorry.

I wasn't sorry that I hadn't talked to him, and I wasn't sorry that Chloe had taken out the battery from the phone he had given me.

I was sorry that I couldn't be there for him, but it wasn't my place anymore. We weren't together.

"I need to see you." Five words that he'd said before, like a record on repeat.

And, each time the words were recited, the same reactions would happen to me internally. The quickness in my breath, the uptick in my heartbeat, and an ache so incredibly strong, it hurt from the inside out.

This time, I understood the cause of my struggle. Above wanting to be with him, I wanted to help him. The weakness inside me was due to the circumstances that had surrounded my mother's death. Her own upward battle was so similar to Hawke's.

"I need my Sunshine."

I sucked in a breath and pulled my knees up close to my chest.

My voice trembled with emotion. "Last time I saw you"—I exhaled deeply—"you were unresponsive, Hawke." I bit the top of my fist, preventing a whimper from escaping. "I thought you were dead."

There was a long pause, an intake of breath, and then, "I'm sorry."

Those two words heated my insides. I jumped up off the bed and started to pace the room, shouting into the phone, "You lied! You said you weren't using. You lied to my face, Hawke."

"I didn't lie," he promised. "That night you saw me was the first time in a long time that I had taken anything." Such conviction and sincerity leaked from his tone that confusion racked my brain.

I clenched my teeth so hard, they ached. I wanted to stick my fingers in my ears and make loud noises to prevent myself from listening because I didn't know what was the truth anymore.

"I needed something to help me forget." His tone begged me to believe him. "Ease my mind. Numb the reality of the truth. I'm sorry. I know what you've been through before . . . with your mom. It was one time, Sunshine. I promise you. One time."

God, I wanted to trust he was being honest, but when it came to Hawke, my clarity meter was all fogged up.

"Sunshine, I need to see you."

"Why?"

I heard it again—the vulnerability in his voice, the slight quiver behind the facade of him trying to keep it together.

"Because you're the only one who's real."

And I weakened.

This was what he did to me. I lost all self-control, all reason.

"Was any of it real?" The words spinning in my brain came out of my mouth even though I hadn't meant to say them aloud.

"What're you talking about?" His voice heightened, on the verge of desperation. "Of fucking course!"

The tension rose. I could feel it in his breathing, his soft, sad demeanor no longer present.

"Alan told me things. About you. About us." A shaky breath escaped me. "Were there others?"

Saying it out loud was like a punch in the stomach, so hard it would have made me topple over.

"Fuck Alan," he grumbled. "Fuck all of them. He's only ever cared about two things—making sure we keep going and that he keeps getting paid."

After a beat, he blew out a breath, and then silence filled the space between us.

"Everything I've felt for you, everything I feel for you now, is real. I love you, Sunshine. I've never lied to you. Ever."

My fragile state was shot. His words and his tone weakened me. I wanted to believe him.

"I need to see you," he begged.

I wondered if he was going to fall apart again. And, if he did, would he turn to his vices, take something for it?

The question on the tip of my tongue finally slipped out. "When was the last time you took anything?"

Here was the moment of truth, a test to see if he could be honest with me.

"Today," he admitted, his voice full of shame.

My lips quivered, and the tears threatened to spill over. Here I was again, in the midst of helping someone battle an addiction. I couldn't save my mom. I most assuredly couldn't save him, as much as I wanted to. I couldn't do this.

"You need help."

"No, I don't," he said, his voice cracking, as though he were at a breaking point. "What I need is you. I need you, Sunshine. I need to see you."

I bit the inside of my cheek, hard enough to stop the feelings coursing through me. "I thought you'd died. I felt it." I stood, my emotions fully on display for him to hear. "I was pounding on your chest, Hawke! Pounding on your chest and screaming your name." The same tears I'd shed that night now fell down my face, only harder. "I thought you were gone, and I'd only ever been that afraid once." Thoughts of my mother flickered in my brain, the pain from the memories was like salt on an open wound. "You need help, Hawke."

I didn't want a repeat of my past. I wouldn't be able to survive it this time around. My mother's death was still fresh, and it hurt. Even with years of counseling, it didn't lessen the toll that it'd taken on me.

"If you love me like you say you love me, then you'll get help." My breathing accelerated, as though I were running and running with no finish line in sight. "Because I care about you, and I'm scared. I can't see you yet, not when you're like this. But, if you get help . . . if you check yourself into rehab, I'll see you."

I inhaled and held it there, waiting to hear what he'd say. He held everything in his one answer.

Seconds ticked by.

One.

Two.

Three.

And then he uttered, "Okay."

The tension oozed out of me in one big exhale.

"But you promise me, Sunshine, you promise me, you'll come see me."

"I promise you." My weak voice lowered to a whisper. "As soon as you check into a facility, I'll be on the next flight."

"You care about me?"

In what seemed like a very long time, I sensed the smile playing at the corner of his lips over the phone.

"Yes. Yes, I do. Very much."

After we hung up, it took me a few minutes to get it together. I plopped on the bed, head in the middle of the mattress, as I stared up at the ceiling, noting the yellow paint chipping off at the sides of the room.

There was a knock on the door, and I sat up, wanting to hit myself.

Josh.

I had forgotten about Josh.

He turned the doorknob and peeked in. "Hey."

"Hey." I turned away, afraid he'd see the torment written on my face. "I'm sorry."

"Don't be. Mind if I come in?"

"No."

He shuffled over, and I scooted, making room for him. His eyes scoured my face, and in that instant, I knew he knew.

"I wanted to check up on you. See if you're okay."

"I'm okay," I said, my voice shaky.

He smiled and then dropped his gaze to my hand before taking it in his. "You're not okay."

A familiar heat spread at our connection, the comfortable touch, the touch I craved.

I looked at our intertwined fingers, reveling in the warmth of his fingertips against mine. "Yeah, that was Hawke." I focused on the window and the apartment building next door.

"You going to go see him?" It wasn't an accusation. His question came out cautious but more sad, like he already knew but only needed me to confirm.

My stomach churned at the complication of my situation. "He's hurting and sick." I knew what Josh was going to say. It was the same thing Chloe had told me—that it wasn't my problem. "He's getting help though."

"And you're going to see him," he said, his voice gentle.

"Josh, he needs help." I wondered why I was defending Hawke. He'd hurt me in more ways than I could count. But, in the next second, I realized it was because he had an addiction. He couldn't help himself. He couldn't see beyond what controlled him—the drugs.

"Would you turn your back on someone who was hurting?"

If anything, Josh and his compassionate heart had to understand.

"Do you love him?" His voice was barely above a whisper.

His question caught me off guard, and I fell silent, taking a moment.

"I do," I told him, holding my breath.

My world stilled to a halt, and my heart stopped in my chest. I didn't want to lose Josh. He'd been my rock when I needed him, but I couldn't shake this overpowering need to see Hawke through to recovery.

"Do you love me?" Josh asked, his eyes full of hope and undeniable sadness.

I wanted to throw myself in his arms, but I knew that wouldn't be fair.

My gaze met his, his eyes solemn. It was as if the air had gotten sucked out of the room in a vacuum, making it hard to breathe.

He was waiting for my reply.

My answer would hurt him, and it was complicated as hell, but I couldn't lie. "I do." My voice cracked around the words, but they were the truth. There was no way you couldn't love Josh because he exuded love himself.

His eyebrows knit together, his thumb tracing the lines of my palm. "Your life is complex, huh?"

I couldn't answer. If I did, I'd burst into tears.

He cleared his throat and stood. "Listen, I have to go . . . stuff to do."

"Okay," I responded, my heart breaking, as he stepped toward my bedroom door.

I followed him out, watching him waver for a moment at the front door. And, just when I thought it would be better for Josh to leave so that I wouldn't complicate his life any further, his next words surprised me.

"It's okay." The pain of heartbreak flickered in his eyes right before he pulled me in. "You know how I feel about you. You don't have to ask me because you already know."

He lightly kissed my temple, and a fluttering sensation initiated in my belly.

Maybe it was something I'd been ignoring because I couldn't face it, but he was right. I knew. It was in Josh's stance, it was in the way he looked at me, it was in the gleam in his eyes every time I walked into the room. It was in the way he would massage my feet when we were watching TV or when he would softly swipe my face that had been kissed by flour as we were baking. It was the small smile and the lingering touches whenever we were next to each other.

Josh was in love with me.

He tipped up my chin to meet my eyes. "You're you, and I can't change you, your desire to save people. I wouldn't want to change you for anything, Princess. But don't lose yourself while saving others, okay?"

I closed my eyes and nodded. He kissed the top of my head before shutting the door behind himself.

A raw ache radiated in the center of my chest because of the struggle within me. It was selfish of me to be thankful for Josh's feelings, but I was. He was the one who had been there for me and kept me together.

I slumped against the wall. There was a sourness in the pit of my stomach at Josh's absence. My eyes stared blankly at the floor, wondering if I could truly save Hawke or if I was only repeating my past and losing myself in the process.

chapter FIVE

MY ARMS WERE ELBOW DEEP in dish soap, rinsing the pan that Josh and I had used to bake cookies. Again. I thanked the God above that I didn't weigh a million pounds, given the amount of baking we'd done lately. Thing was, baking calmed me. It gave me purpose, and it kept me from worrying about Hawke.

A week had passed since Hawke agreed to seek help.

When I'd looked up the Pure Serenity Rehabilitation Center, the facility he had picked online, I'd had to double-check to verify that it was a drug and alcohol rehabilitation center. It seemed more like a resort with its endless recreational activities, like waterskiing and the kayaking. Let's not forget about the infinity pool and the full-service spa.

If I hadn't understood the treacherous road ahead of him, the uphill battle he'd face to fight this addiction, I would've wanted to go to that place as well.

I stared at the phone on the counter, my nerves on edge. The headlines from the morning entertainment news indicated that Hawke had checked into rehab, but the sources were unsure about what. There was speculation about drug addiction, and some even thought it was sexual addiction. I had known he was going in because we had decided on the phone which facility was best for him. What I hadn't counted on was the media outlets getting wind that he was going on the day he was checking in.

I wished I could shield him from the world sometimes, but that was impossible when I was miles away.

When the cell vibrated against the cream countertop, I almost pounced on it, barely wiping my hands on my jeans before I picked it up. "Hello?"

"Hey, Sunshine."

My whole body tensed at the strain in Hawke's voice.

"Hawke, how are you?" I rubbed my one hand down my pant leg and rapidly blinked while anxiety of the unknown rose within me.

"I'm here. They're about to take this phone. Part of their protocol. I won't be able to talk to you until the week's over. You're going to come see me though, right?" The desperation in his tone hit me straight in my chest.

"I'll be there on Saturday," I said without hesitation.

I had promised him, and I would pull through. People battling addiction needed support, and Hawke had only me.

He released a long sigh, like seeing me was all that mattered. What mattered to me was that he got better.

"I hate these types of places. Their bare walls make me feel claustrophobic, like I'm in a fucking jail cell. Or worse, a psych ward."

Hawke's name was true to his being; he was a free bird. No one could cage him in.

"You don't like pools and daily spa treatments?" I joked, trying to lighten the mood.

"It's not like that here, Sunshine. It's not."

I leaned over the sink, pressing my hand against the counter. He wouldn't survive this week without motivation, without assurance.

"It's only for three months," I reminded him. "I'll be there to spend time with you almost every weekend."

Silence.

Forever silence.

I closed my eyes and prayed to the heavens above that this would work, that rehab would help him.

"I want you to get well, Hawke," I whispered. "You promised me you'd take me to Paris, remember? How is that going to happen if you aren't well?"

Muffled voices echoed in his room before he said, "Tilton has your itinerary. I'll see you on Saturday, Sunshine."

"All right," I said, forcing my voice to stay even. "See you soon."

I held the phone, staring at Hawke's face on the screen saver. It was a side profile. I'd randomly snapped it when he was sitting on the couch, doing nothing. Even then, he looked beautiful.

He will get through this, I told myself over and over. I'd be his anchor.

THE AROMA OF FRESH PASTA filtered through the air. Oregano, pepper, garlic.

Chloe and Josh were in a full-on cook-off. Chloe's and Josh's mothers were Italian and lived on pastas and breads and flavorful sauces. I guessed they were big into food. With Chloe, it was always competition, so she had challenged Josh to a cooking competition.

My counter was filled with pasta flour, the pasta shredder, and multiple gadgets. It was *Top Chef* but in my kitchen.

Me? I was plopped on the kitchen table, pretending to putz around on my computer, when, in reality, Josh and Chloe were my evening entertainment.

It had been almost four whole days since I'd last spoken to Hawke. It was as if I were waiting for the first day of school from the nervous bubbling in my chest, the nonstop thinking of everything, and the never-ending insomnia.

Forty-eight more hours. All the anticipation was leading to Saturday when Tilton would pick me up, and we'd drive to Schaumburg's private airport to fly down to Phoenix where I'd finally visit Hawke after not seeing him in such a long time.

I wondered how he was doing. The hardest part of rehab was those first few days. Though I'd never experienced an addiction withdrawal, I'd been told that the pain was horrible. When day three had hit, I'd relaxed a little bit more. He'd made it through three days, and he'd just have to do it day by day. When I saw him, I'd make sure to boost him up and give him the encouragement he needed to keep on trekking along to the finish line. I'd come every weekend if work would allow it. I'd see him through this.

Chloe's animated tone broke me from my thoughts.

"Aha! That's not how you flatten the dough." Chloe's cheeks, nose, and one eye were white, like she'd been kissed by the flour.

Josh was wearing his Cubs hat backward, and his sleeves were rolled up to his shoulders. "And here I thought, it was about the ingredients." He glanced over at me and winked.

Chloe pointed a scolding finger his way. "You! You're flirting with the judge!"

"No, I'm not." His face feigned innocence.

She jumped up and down. "Yes, you so were." Then, she started to wink in my direction. "What is this?" Wink, wink, wink. "Is that not flirting?"

He tipped his head in my direction, his hands flattening out the dough in front of him. "Can you blame me? Look at her."

Laughter bubbled from my chest. "I'm staying strictly unbiased, flirting or not. I'm judging on look, taste, and texture."

A Yahoo alert flashed on my computer screen. The caption of the picture read, *Hawke Calvin left Pure Serenity Rehabilitation Center this morning.*

My heart immediately dropped. I blinked, unbelieving. He'd left? Already?

The rest of the article was blurred into a bunch of words. My only focus was on Hawke's face. I couldn't read his eyes because he was wearing his signature black Ray-Bans. Tilton was holding the door open to the limo as Hawke was stepping in.

Visible tremors shook my hands as fear knotted my insides.

"Sam!"

I jumped, glancing up at a curious Chloe, and then I slammed my laptop shut.

Through all my shock, I hadn't heard Chloe yelling my name.

I cleared my throat, trying to get a grip. "So, are you guys going to take turns using the rack to dry your pasta?"

"What's wrong?" Chloe asked, rinsing her hands. "What was on the computer?"

"Nothing." I scrunched my face. I wished I had been born a better liar or had even a little of the liar gene so that I could keep a straight face.

She cocked her head toward Josh, and they shared a knowing look. As though she had telepathic powers, she immediately went for the remote.

"No!" I said.

But she beat me to it. She flipped the television to the entertainment channel, and just like that, Hawke's face was plastered on the screen.

"Hawke Calvin, the lead singer of Def Deception, walked out of rehab today. He became irate with one of the staff members and left the facility. Although nothing has been confirmed, it's said he entered rehab for alcohol and drug addiction."

A second later, my phone rang on the table. Chloe and I glanced at each other before she leaped at the table and grabbed it. I fell onto her, and we both tumbled to the floor in a large thud.

She held the phone with both hands pressed to her chest while I battled her for it. I heard Josh calling our names, but I didn't care. My main focus was on the phone.

"Let go!" I screeched. Desperation to speak to Hawke, to know the reasons he'd left, and to know he was okay tore through me.

"No," she growled. "Fucker is not talking to you. Ever. Fat chance."

We thrashed around, four hands gripping the same device. Her caramel-brown locks hit me in the face, giving me hair burn.

Just when I had a firm handle on the phone, Chloe flipped over onto her stomach. "Hello?" she said, answering it.

My throat closed up when she stood, her face beet red from our struggle.

"What do you want?" she asked.

"Chloe," I begged, pushing myself to stand.

"Nope. No. It's not happening, buddy." She raised a palm to stop me. "Sam sees the good in everyone. It's in her genetic makeup. And she wants to see the good in you, but you know what you are? You're toxic." Her nostrils flared, and her eyes turned hard. "A damn leech that drains the blood out of every human thing it touches, and I will not let you drain her, you fucker. Stop calling her. You had your chance, and you fucked up over and over again. She's done loving you!" And then she hung up the phone and chucked it across the room.

The impact of the phone against the hard wood floor had the battery disconnecting from the cell.

When I eyed the silver phone against the floor, her finger shook in my direction. "Don't you dare. You're done! You hear me? Done! Done! Done!"

My jaw clenched. The tension in the room was at an all-time high. We stared at each other, unblinking, unmoving. Her shoulders strained. Her chin rose.

"You're never going to speak to him. Ever." She glared. "Or we're done."

I flinched. I knew she was angry, and I knew she didn't mean it, but still . . . it hurt.

Our staring contest seemed to last forever, as though we were battling in a non-blinking contest, until Josh's voice broke our connection.

"Guys."

We both glanced over to him. He was standing in the kitchen, holding his pasta midair. I had forgotten he was still here.

"You done?" He quirked an eyebrow. "'Cause I'm pretty sure we're not done."

I blinked, stunned for a moment. Josh being Josh, he was trying to ease the strain in the air.

Chloe tilted her head and stared at Josh in the strangest way. Then, her shoulders relaxed, and the corners of her mouth tipped upward. She let out a low laugh. "You know I'm still kicking your ass in the cook-off."

The mood lightened between them, and I forced myself to let this go. She'd just been trying to protect me.

When I approached her, she brought me into a hug and held me fiercely. I wrapped my arms around her just as tightly. I couldn't lose her. In some ways, she was all I had.

She spoke softly, "I know you want to save everyone. Cats up in trees, stray dogs, but you can't. It's been a while since you've seen him, and you're getting better. I don't want you to start at zero again, okay?" She pulled back and searched my face. The same pleading eyes that had begged me not to blame myself many years ago bore into mine. "You can't help people if they don't want to help themselves. We know this, Sam."

I nodded.

Usually, I was the mama bear, helping her through her issues with guys and whatnot. Lately, it seemed like our roles had reversed. It felt oddly refreshing. Like someone was taking care of me instead of the other way around.

I blew out a breath and buried my head into her chest, taking in her comfort. She was right. I couldn't live like this. I had to put a stop to the emotional merry-go-round.

chapter SIX

WINTER SWOOPED IN. SNOW COVERED the ground, and below-zero temperatures forced out the thick down jackets.

My days were filled with work and waiting for my culinary school acceptance letters to come back. I would check my mail twice a day, hoping and wishing to see Le Cordon Bleu's reply.

And my nights were filled with Chloe and Josh. They made sure that I never wavered from my I'm-done promise. It was hard not to watch TV or turn on the radio to check on how Hawke was doing, but there was never a dull moment.

Tonight, Chloe had a marketing event, so I'd accompanied Josh to his family's mega mansion.

I peeked up from the dining room table, noting the high windows that spanned the whole wall behind him. The manicured hedges and rolling greens were covered with snow. The wall paper and crown molding made me feel like I was in a high-end architectural magazine. Though my surroundings overwhelmed me, my company made me feel oddly at home.

I sat back, taking in the scent of coffee filtering through the air, as my tiramisu was being torn apart. Not a crumb was left on my plate.

Albert, Josh's dad, had said something to make his daughter laugh, and I studied their interaction. Their family functioned happily without the weight of their grandfather. The only good thing about their dear old grandpa was that he didn't live nearby.

"You didn't like your dessert?" Josh tilted his head toward my empty plate.

"Yeah. Worst cake ever." I scrunched my face, and he laughed. Though, honestly, I could've made a better tiramisu at home.

He pushed his plate toward me. "Here, Princess. All yours."

Josh was the epitome of kindness, always so giving, when I felt like I gave nothing back.

I pushed his plate back in his direction. "It's okay."

He stared at me for a moment before both dimples popped up on display. His eyes reminded me of dark cocoa beans.

My curiosity piqued. "Do you look like your mom?"

Albert spoke up, "Yes. Carbon copy. From those dimples to the curl in his hair to his personality. He is his mother's son through and through." Albert peered up at his son, as though he were a trophy. "His sense of humor, too." His voice was full of pride.

"Aw, shucks." Josh ducked his head, feigning shyness.

I laughed.

"Dad, tell Sam how you and Mom met." Casey scooted to the edge of her seat, her eyes bright. "I make him tell this story to everyone who hasn't heard it yet because it's the sweetest thing." She rested her elbows on the table and leaned in. "I wished Robert's and my story was as romantic." She sighed wistfully.

"Really, Case?" Josh asked.

She motioned with her hands. "Yes, Dad. Now, go." She knocked on the dining table, her eyes expectantly waiting on her father.

"We were at a sandwich shop." A slight smile touched Albert's lips. "I was with my buddies, and she was ordering in front of us. She was strikingly beautiful. Drop-dead gorgeous." His eyes twinkled with an inner glow as he recalled the memory. "Lucky for me, the two guys with me already had girlfriends. Well, she ordered a meatball sub with sugar on top."

Josh laughed beside me. "Mother had a crazy sweet tooth." He pointed to himself. "Just like me."

"She had to repeat it a few times because the server thought he had heard her wrong. She repeated it loud and clear the second time, and when he laughed, she shrugged and said, 'What's wrong with wanting everything sweet?' And then she brought out her coin purse and proceeded to pay for her three-dollar sandwich with change."

Deep chuckles escaped him. "I stepped in, thinking I was all debonair and suave, and threw a ten at the guy at the register. She swiped at my hand and gave me the look of death. Anyone else would've been frightened. But, to me, she looked like a kitten pretending to be a lion."

His facial features fell, his eyes staring, unfocused at the table. "She told me she didn't need my money, and if I really wanted to help, I should help her count her pennies. And so I did." He touched his hand to his heart. "That's how I knew I was in love."

"Why was she paying with coins?" I asked.

"She told me she saved her dollars to deposit at the bank. She paid for food with her coins." His gaze became unfocused, and his smile faltered.

"We talked for hours that night. I loved listening to her. She had the most beautiful voice and animated face. While she was telling me her life story, I was wondering how I could get this girl to marry me." His voice turned quiet. "I didn't want the night to end. My friends had left, and the sandwich shop was about to close up. I'd never been nervous about asking girls out before, but Kathy . . . she was different."

He stared at his napkin, hard, like he was reliving the moment. "And then I manned up and asked her out, but she denied me, telling me she didn't want to date until she was done with school. I asked her if she meant high school or college. Not that it mattered because I would've waited forever for her." He lifted his eyes and scanned our faces. "She said she hadn't decided yet when she would be ready for dating."

A sad smile touched his lips. "I panicked when it was time to leave, and I asked her for her number, which she refused to give me. Grasping at straws, I asked her when she'd be back at the sandwich shop. She told me it was her regular stop every Wednesday after class. So, every Wednesday after school, I would be there, helping her count her pennies."

The table turned silent, and the mood became somber. I could feel how much they missed her. It was in Casey's glossed over eyes and in Josh's slight smile as he focused on his father.

"She sounds like a wonderful woman," I said.

"She was. She was . . . she was my person. My soul mate." Albert let out a long sigh and stood. His eyes misted from the memory of her. "Excuse me for a minute."

After he walked out of the dining room, Casey ran after him. Josh's stare dropped to the table, his eyes glossed over.

I touched his hand, breaking him from his trance. "It's a beautiful memory."

"It is." He picked up a crumb from the table and flicked it to the side. "Casey loves hearing it." He blew out a breath. "But, why does she put him through that?"

I knew why. "Because that's all she has of her mother, Josh. Memories."

If I had someone to tell me stories of my mom, I'd ask them to repeat them over and over again. It had been only my mom and me and the dad I never talked to anymore.

His eyebrows pulled together, as though he were contemplating. "Sometimes, I wonder if memories, even happy ones, are a good thing when she's dead."

"You can't think of it like that."

His eyes met mine, and he tightened his hold on my hand. "Yeah, but memories only remind you of what you once had, of how happy you used to be. I don't know if I can be that guy who lives in his past."

I leaned my head against his shoulder, wanting to take his pain, even for just a second.

When I thought of my mother and all the happy times we'd shared, I couldn't imagine not having those memories to get me through the tough days.

But there was some truth to what Josh was saying.

And, when I thought of Hawke, Josh's words never rang truer.

I needed to let go of my past and move into the future.

THE DOORBELL RANG, AND MY stomach jumped to my throat. I flattened my hands against my half-slip black silk dress that lay mid thigh, and then I put on one last coat of mascara before glancing back at myself in the mirror.

Chloe had curled my hair to perfection and had pulled back half of it from my face into a beautiful waterfall braid. I swore, she needed to work part-time as a hairdresser and makeup artist or a personal shopper.

I ran into the living room, noticing that Chloe was watching her favorite show. "Thanks for getting the door," I sassed.

"Sorry, I'm just so engrossed in all that is Jamie Fraser." She exhaled an exaggerated sigh.

I laughed. "Yeah, yeah."

I pulled open the door and blinked. My mouth might have dropped open, too.

Josh was standing in front of me, all six feet of hotness and all GQ. I blew out a silent breath. *God, he was handsome.* Not that I hadn't noticed before. But with his black fitted suit pants replacing his jeans, the sharp suit jacket and snug white button-down replacing his usual T-shirt, and his styled hair no longer covered with a hat, he looked magazine-worthy gorgeous.

A blush touched my cheeks, and I sucked in a breath because he had totally caught me gawking.

His fist flew to his mouth before he turned to walk away and then flipped back, strolling toward me. "Hot damn, girl. You look . . . you look . . . wow."

The flush on my cheeks heated to Crayola crayon pink. "You and your lines," I said, trying to calm my racing heart.

"Let me try a different approach." He slowly walked toward me.

With each of his steps forward, goose bumps prickled my skin. I was aware of his whole proximity, of all of him, more than I ever had been.

He towered over me, rested one arm over the doorframe, crossed his ankles, and angled closer. "Hey."

His face was so serious, but his moves were super corny, like he was on some movie set from the fifties. I couldn't help but laugh out loud.

"Hey," I replied, moving to make room to let him pass. "We're late."

I reached for his arm and pulled him in the door. He almost tripped, staggering inside. His suave demeanor disappeared from the abrupt movement.

I wanted to laugh again, but if we didn't leave in about two seconds, we'd be late for the ceremony, and I wanted to see Candice walking down the aisle.

"My shoes, my shoes!" I scoured the living room for the black pumps with red bows. I swore, I'd seen them in here just a few days ago.

Chloe tilted her head, and a strange look spread on her face. "What did you say they looked like?"

I threw my hands in the air as Josh chuckled behind me.

"They had bows, Chloe!"

She hit her forehead and stood from the couch. "I wore those yesterday. Duh!" She laughed like it was no big deal that she hadn't just taken my new shoes that I'd bought specifically for Candice's wedding.

"Really?" I asked, incredulous.

Emerging from her bedroom, she found them in a snap and swaggered over to me, the straps swinging on her two fingers.

"Wow." I shook my head.

My best friend seriously had no tact. Yes, we practically shared everything, but there had to be a line drawn somewhere.

"At least she broke them in for you," Josh said, making Chloe laugh. "Made them easier to walk in?"

Always a silver lining with this boy.

Chloe threw him a thumbs-up. "See? At the end of it all, I'm looking out for you." She lifted her toes and wiggled them. "I've got blisters to prove it."

I rolled my eyes in exaggeration.

Josh offered his arm, and I used his bicep to steady myself as I slipped my feet into the four-inch stilettos.

When I stood steady, Josh let out a low whistle.

Chloe clapped and did a little jump. "Damn, you look hot. Hold up, so I can take a picture of you two. It looks like you're going to a red-carpet event."

Josh wrapped one arm around my lower back and pulled me into him. I felt his fingertips press against my waist and his minty soft breath against my temple. I angled closer to get a whiff of his cologne. He never wore cologne. There was a hint of sweetness and a touch of spice. It was intoxicating—the scent of him and the nearness of him.

Chloe held up her phone and I smiled.

When I peered up at Josh, my breath caught. He was staring directly at me, no smile on his face, and his eyes held a certain emotion I couldn't place.

I cleared my throat. "Okay, let's get going, or we'll miss one of my favorite parts—when she enters the church."

He nodded, his usual joking self gone. He intertwined our fingers. For the first time since he'd reached for my hand in the shoe department to check out my palm, nervous butterflies stirred in my stomach, the calmness from his touch not there.

Lately, I'd been sensing that things between us were shifting. It was in his intense gaze when we were watching TV or baking. It was in his lingering touches or his need to touch me when I simply passed by him. The world around me was changing—or more, *our* world was. And, for once, I wanted to see where it would lead.

We walked out the door, hand in hand. Josh only released me to open the passenger car door.

The drive would take forty-five minutes, but as I stayed quiet, the radio playing in the background, I realized this was one of the reasons I enjoyed his company. There were no forced conversations, no fakeness to fill the air. It was just him and me in the silence. A comfortable silence. Yes, the banter was there, but sometimes, it wasn't, and that was okay.

When we parked at the parking lot of the church in St. Charles, Josh rushed to open my door. I stepped out, pulling in the long winter-white peacoat that Chloe had lent me. The frigid air nipped at my skin. The frosty wind brushed against my bare legs.

After slipping my hand through Josh's, we headed inside.

I couldn't help but gawk at the church's beauty. Deep red and orange stained glass adorned the windows. I tipped my head back, appreciating the colors against the blue sky above us. The gray bricked structure steepled to a peak, pointing to the heavens.

"Gosh, this church is so beautiful. I love the architecture."

"Yeah." He nodded. "My mom and dad got married at a small church—another way to piss off my grandparents. They wanted a big wedding for their only son, and my mother wanted simple and just the two of them."

I tightly squeezed his hand. Every time he talked about his mom, there was a sense of sadness in his eyes but also great joy. It was funny how you could reminisce about the good when someone was gone even though their absence could still bring you grief.

As we walked up the sidewalk, he continued, "I'll have to take you there sometime. It's in a tiny suburb, about two hours outside of Manhattan."

"I'd love to go there," I said honestly.

"There are six pews, and the most elaborate thing inside the church is the altar, which is a thick slab of wood with the cross sitting in the center."

I swung our hands together. "It sounds amazing. It's the little things that give a place character." A small thrill rushed through my skin. I enjoyed seeing bits and pieces of Josh's life.

He released me when he opened the door, but once we were inside, his hand went into mine, like magnets meant to unite.

"Yes, it is. The little things," he said quietly.

My free hand flew to my chest as I lifted my eyes to take everything in. The exterior did not do the church justice. More stained glass windows lined the walls, and the vaulted ceiling had detailed paintings of angels and clouds. My heels clip-clopped against the marble floor as Josh led me down the aisle. We rushed to sit down, and once we did, Pachelbel's Canon in D began to play in the background.

When the doors opened and the congregation stood, I tiptoed to see if I could get a good peek at Candice. I saw the top of her hair bunched in beautiful dark curls, but I couldn't see her face. She walked with her usual bounce but with grace, as though she were floating on air. I caught a glimpse of her father when they passed us, his eyes red from tears.

And then I saw her.

She looked exquisite.

Her white apron was now replaced with a stunning white gown. The beaded trumpet dress hugged the contours of her body until mid hip and then gradually widened to the hem. A trail four feet long was being towed behind her.

My lips quivered, and when I saw the brightness in her eyes and the smile on her face as she stared directly down the aisle to the man she was going to spend the rest of her life with, I lost it. I swiped at my tears, ecstatic and beyond happy for my friend.

She was beauty personified.

Strong, warm hands wrapped around my waist and pulled me back against a chest.

I peered up at Josh, a little embarrassed that he'd seen me shed tears. "I'm such a sap."

He chuckled. "Nothing wrong with that." He extended his hand and offered a light-red handkerchief.

"Where did you get this?" I asked, slightly amused.

"My suit pocket."

"Oh, I didn't even notice. I didn't think boys carried these anymore."

"Boys probably don't," he said in a tone like another line was coming. But he was serious and sweet. "Men, yes. Plus, what can I say? I'm old school."

I blew my nose, snot and all, and he made a face.

"Yeah, you can totally keep that," he said.

When Candice and Jerry faced each other and recited their traditional vows, claiming to love each other through sickness and health, in good times and in bad, I teared up again.

When Josh offered me another handkerchief, I turned toward him, eyes wide. "Where are you getting all of these?"

And that was when he pulled out another one from the inside of his suit pocket, like a clown with endless silk coming from his sleeve.

He shrugged and faced the front of the church.

After Candice and Jerry kissed and were pronounced husband and wife, the congregation cheered. Josh cupped his hands around his mouth and hollered.

When they walked down the aisle, followed by the wedding party, I slipped my arm through Josh's and swaggered out with them to the "Wedding March."

The sun was shining brightly, beating down on us, like God was in agreement and showering his blessing down on them. I smiled big, knowing everything was right in the world.

Chaos surrounded Candice, and I doubted my ability to squeeze through her family and friends to congratulate her.

So, I pointed my thumb toward the car. "Reception?"

"Yes, let's." He grinned. "Your carriage—also known as the Beemer—awaits."

I laughed, not remembering the last time I felt this happy. "Let's go, my Prince Charming."

He chuckled. "That, I am, babe. That, I am."

chapter SEVEN

AS I SAT BACK, FULLY satisfied with my dinner, I took in the decor of the reception hall. I'd noticed it when I first arrived, but I'd been too hungry to really appreciate the touches of Candice everywhere.

Every table was adorned with a tall arrangement of peonies, and aside from the black table linens and black silk chair covers, everything was tastefully done in different arrays of blushes, light pinks, and deep pinks. The signing table was decorated with their pictures in pink-ribboned frames, and even the straws for our drinks were pink.

The moment I had introduced Josh to my coworkers, they started chatting it up, and Josh being Josh, he was making the table laugh.

For a brief second, a second I wanted to take away, I thought of Hawke. If I had brought him tonight, it would've been a totally different experience. He'd have been more reserved, standoffish. Not on purpose, but he wasn't comfortable around people who weren't his in-crowd, people who didn't know him.

I blew out a breath as I watched Josh cracking up so hard, he was holding his stomach.

If Hawke had come with me, the whole wedding would've revolved around him. I could imagine everyone begging for his autograph. Instead of taking pictures of the bride, they'd have been taking pictures of the famous rock star.

"Sammy!"

I looked up to see Candice behind me, carrying her train in one hand. Her new husband trailed behind her. I stood, strolled toward her, and gave my girlie pie the biggest soul-crushing sous-chef-to-sous-chef hug. Then, I pulled back to take her in.

At the church and from far away, I could only get glimpses of her, but now, up close, I realized she looked absolutely breathtaking. "You look so beautiful. And this place . . . this reception"—I swept my hand around the room—"is so you." I motioned to Jerry. "And you, too, of course."

I jumped into another hug, and she squeezed me back equally hard.

"Who is the hottie?" she said, peering over me.

"That's Josh." I quirked an eyebrow.

Of course I'd known Josh long enough that all my coworkers had heard his name being thrown around here and there.

"That is Josh?" She fanned herself. "Talk about J.Crew rolled into one tall, dark, and handsome."

I playfully slapped Candice's arm. Her husband was one step away from her.

Jerry cleared his throat. "Hey, Sam." He smiled warmly.

"Oh, please. He knows me well enough by now to know that I truly only have eyes for him." Candice slipped her hand through his arm and tiptoed to kiss him on the lips. "Anyway, are you going to introduce me? Are you two dating?"

"I don't know." Because I didn't. All I knew was that we were starting to feel like more than friends.

She released her husband and grabbed my hand. She was heading right where I'd expected her to—straight to my table and Josh.

"No!" I tugged her back, stopping mid step. "Don't embarrass me, Candice!"

When Josh saw the woman in a white dress and her husband coming over, he stood. "Hey," he said, sticking out his hand. "Congrats."

Candice pulled him into a hug. "I'm a hugger today because I'm the bride. I'm Candice." She stepped back and smiled, showing off her Crest strip whites.

"I'm Josh."

"I know." She laughed.

I already felt a blush climbing up my cheeks.

"I've heard your name a handful of times. So"—she clicked her tongue on the roof of her mouth—"what's going on between you two?" She motioned between Josh and me with her pointer finger.

I swore, my face burned as bright as the red bows on my black pumps.

"Candice!" I swatted at her hand, and she swatted me right back.

Throwing an arm over my shoulder, she pulled me in by my neck. "See this chick right here?" She tilted her head to touch mine. "She's way too good for rock stars, so whatever you're doing, you'd better have good intentions. So, what's going on here?"

A dimple emerged on Josh's cheek. His look turned serious, as though he were contemplating his next words. Then, he said tenderly, "She's my girl. I'm just waiting for her to realize that."

"Good answer, Josh. Good answer."

My eyes locked with his, brown to brown, but his were a darker shade while mine were a flat color. The longer he stared at me, the more my heart fluttered wildly in my chest.

The DJ interrupted our gaze, announcing the first dance with Candice and Jerry.

Candice turned to walk toward the dance floor but not before she gave Josh a fake death stare. "But I'm watching you. So, don't mess up, buddy."

"At Last" by Etta James cooed through the speakers. Jerry extended his hand, and Candice took it, curtsying in her Southern way. While they danced, Josh stepped toward me, but I focused on the newlyweds, trying to calm the heat emanating from my cheeks.

He moved into my line of sight, and I played it off as coolly as I could. "So, I'm your girl now?"

He rubbed his jaw, his look thoughtful. "You've been my girl since the day I slipped that glass slipper onto your foot. You've just been slow on the uptake." He shrugged, giving me a sweet smile that almost broke my heart.

"Your lines," I said, playing it off, as I shook my head. The back of my hand flew to the top of my forehead. "I can't take the lines anymore. It's just too much," I cooed in an exaggerated tone. "Your dimples and your rock-hard body and your lines." I leaned back in a pretend faint moment.

Now, it was his turn to turn red.

He pulled my hand down and held it between us. "Rock-hard body, huh?"

My pulse leaped at the electricity that surged between us, the softness of his fingers stroking the side of my wrist, the scent of his masculine cologne filling my senses. My breathing slowed, and my lips parted at his proximity.

I gulped. Barely keeping my voice even, I said, "It's hard not to notice when you're always strolling into my apartment after basketball, shirtless and a hot, sweaty mess."

He swallowed hard this time, his eyes piercing mine. "Maybe it looks rock hard, but you can't tell until you touch it." He tugged me forward, placing my hand on the top of his button-down.

My hands moistened, and a delightful shiver coursed through my veins. For the first time, I yearned to touch him. My hand dropped lower from his chest, trailing down to his abdomen.

His lips parted, and he held his breath. He stared at me with an intensity that seared through me.

"Josh," I whispered.

A fast song broke our quiet connection, and before I knew what was happening, a blur of white was dragging me to the dance floor, forcing me to dance to Justin Timberlake. Candice's smile overrode everyone else's in the room. Happiness exuded from her every pore as she belted out Justin's lyrics and took my hands, swinging them to the beat of the bass.

I turned around, and my gaze locked with Josh's. In one hand, he held a beer bottle as he chatted it up with my coworkers, Jim and Todd. The great thing about Josh was that he was social. I didn't feel the need to see if he was okay because I knew he was.

When a medley of Michael Jackson's songs came through the speakers, Josh swaggered over to the dance floor, curling one finger in a come-hither motion. I laughed as he flicked his foot back and forth in a signature Michael move.

"Let's dance, beautiful."

I wrinkled my nose. "I don't think so."

Ignoring me, he gripped my hand and tugged us to the middle of the dance floor. His hands fell to my hips as he swayed them to the music, and I laughed at his antics.

He was no singer, and his voice was horrendous, but he was belting out Michael Jackson like he was the famous singer himself. I stepped back and watched in awe as he started to moonwalk. Within a few seconds, a crowd formed around him, cheering him on. He did the pelvic thrust in the middle of the circle, and I laughed so hard, I might have peed a little.

Josh sang *Beat It*, using his fist as his mic.

He sang loud and proud like he was giving his own personal concert. He ended his performance with one hand on his pelvis while his other hand flew to tip down his head.

The people around us roared to a deafening cheer, and then he bowed in the cutest Josh way. When he approached me, he was breathless, and I clapped my hands, thoroughly entertained.

"Bravo! You can be on *So You Think You Can Dance*, but don't try out for *The Voice* anytime soon."

He laughed, and the tune changed, a slow melody playing in the background. I recognized the artist belting out her soulful tunes in "Make You Feel My Love." It was Adele.

A dimple flashed on his cheek, and when he stopped a few steps in front of me, he held out his hand. "May I have this dance?"

It reminded me of prom, the way he extended his hand in a gentlemanlike gesture. And, in grade school fashion, my heart pitter-pattered in my chest.

We'd held hands, almost everyday, yet I was nervous to hold his hand this time. When he took another step forward, the fluttering in my chest intensified at his proximity.

I scrunched up my face. "I don't dance," I joked.

"Liar." Both of his boyish dimples were on display.

And, when I placed my hand in his, an electric current passed through me. The air shifted between us as our eyes locked. The familiar longing spread through his features, but what was different was my mirrored look of desire that reflected through his eyes.

He intertwined our fingers, bringing me closer. Slowly, his fingers flexed and wrapped around my hand. He pulled me into him and wrapped his arms around me in a tight vise until we were nearly one. My softness pushed against his hardness, and I rested my head against his chest. He smelled like his aftershave, cologne, and all man.

Josh's hold was all-consuming. Every nerve in my body was on edge as we swayed to the soulful melody of Adele. I had a strong awareness of our bodies pressing together, our joined hands against his heart and his free hand on the small of my back.

After a moment, my eyes fell shut, and all my senses heightened. It was like when you disabled sight, your sense of hearing, sound, and touch intensified.

The thump of his heart warmed my hand, the scent of his aftershave wafting into my nose. His uneven hot breaths brushed against my cheek, sending goose bumps to travel down my neck. His fingertips branded themselves against my hip, tightened, and brought me closer, flush against his lean, hard body. He held me as if he were never going to let me go.

For a moment, just a moment, we were the only ones in the

room. Like we were in a slow globe and everyone else was looking in.

A soft exhale escaped from his lips. With his light fingertips, he lifted my chin. I opened my eyes and stared into the warmth, the brown reminding me of a dark chocolate river, endless and inviting.

His eyes flickered to my lips, and my insides quivered with want and fear because here I was again, the girl who'd fallen too deeply.

Maybe I was already where he was. Maybe Chloe had been right all along, and I'd been in denial because what I felt was so familiar—a deep-rooted ache in the center of my chest.

"I want to kiss you," he breathed. He sucked in his bottom lip as the desire and longing in his eyes poured out of him.

"You never asked before."

Because he never had. Not in the alley. Not before his so-called friendly kiss in front of Hawke.

"Because this time . . . this time is different." His voice lowered, husky and serious. The one-liner goofy Josh was no longer present.

My breath caught in my throat at the adoring look in his eyes, as though I were the most beautiful and only woman in the universe. I swallowed hard at what I saw—the longing, the hunger, and most of all, the love.

He didn't need to ask because there was no way I could deny him when I very much wanted the same thing.

I lifted my chin in answer, and once our lips connected, heat spread, radiating from my chest to the rest of my limbs.

His kiss was gentle, but it knocked the wind out of me. His kiss packed a punch like I had ever experienced. I melted into him, giving myself to the passion of his kiss.

He loved me. There was no doubt. He loved me with all of his being, and in that moment, in the silence, I knew I'd fallen for him, too. Fallen for his kindness, fallen for his truth, but most of all, fallen for his heart.

There was no denying the lightness in my limbs and the warmth in my chest, all caused from his arms and lips on me.

I was in love with Josh Stanton.

This was our first kiss, and I knew it was a kiss that would lead to forever.

chapter EIGHT

AFTER THAT MOMENT, IT WAS like Josh had branded me for an eternity. His arms were pressed against my sides, caging me in, and we danced until we were the last ones standing. Even the bride and groom had left.

It was midnight when we hopped into his car. His lips met mine at every stoplight, every Stop sign, until he was parked in front of his apartment. His mouth covered mine with a deep-rooted hunger. We were connected by lips or hands or arms until we made our way into his place.

What had started as a slow-building love affair had accelerated into a fast-moving train ride that I had no doubt would end the night in an explosion of ecstasy.

His hands groped me through my dress as he led us to his bedroom, never breaking his hold. My body was on fire, my face flushed, my nipples pebbling and scraping against the inside of my bra.

I should stop it, press the brakes, but we had waited so long. And, as much as I sensed he needed me, I longed for him more.

After stepping out of my shoes, I slipped off his jacket and undid his tie. He pulled back, lust filling his hooded eyes. My fingers undid each and every button as our lips connected again. The delicious taste of him had wetness pooling between my legs.

His kisses slowed, becoming gentle and deliberate, and he pulled back and met my eyes, walking me backward to the bed. The way he studied me, it was as if he were committing every detail to memory.

"I've waited so long for this—for you," he breathed.

His fingers dropped to my waist, the touch of his hand almost unbearable in tenderness. It was agonizing torture because my hunger for him was too much.

With his free hand, he brushed against my cheek, the light touch igniting me from the inside out. My heart was beating like a sledgehammer inside my chest.

My eyes fell shut, and his mouth made contact with mine. The kisses were sweet, innocent, reverent. They were different than the other times we'd kissed. He kissed me as if he were breathing life out of me and into himself.

His shaky finger trailed to the nape of my neck, down my shoulder, up to the back of my head, threading through my hair.

My insides were soaring as his tongue traced the fullness of my mouth before licking the seam of my lips. Our tongues collided, intertwining, and I moaned, rocking against him, feeling his hardness lengthen by my thigh.

Without breaking contact, he lifted me, and I wrapped my legs around his waist. My breathing accelerated as he kissed me deeply, digging his fingertips into the silk of my dress, which hugged me like an itchy barrier between us.

When he stilled and gently eased me onto the bed, he released our kiss. I peered up at him as he cupped the side of my cheek. There were a slew of emotions in his eyes—affection, passion, need—but one emotion that had me holding my breath was love.

"Sam . . ." My name was uttered with such adoration.

His eyes held a vulnerability in them, and I knew, if I crossed this line and it wasn't permanent, his heart would break.

There was no going back. I had to be sure this was what I wanted.

But, looking into his eyes, I knew I wanted him. I wanted forever. I wasn't made for rock stars and fantasies. I was a small-town girl. I craved stability and a love that would last a lifetime. Maybe I had tricked myself before, thinking that was what I wanted, but it wasn't who I was at my core.

After one soft exhale, I closed the gap between us and kissed him. "I love you," I said breathlessly because he had to know I felt the same.

His whole body melted into me, and I sensed his relief, as though that were all he'd been waiting for.

Then, my fingers moved to his waistband. One button and then two. But he stopped my hands and pulled back, his eyes smoldering. My insides shivered with nervousness. He had a strange look on his face, a look of carnal hunger. And, if I thought I had been breathless before . . . I was even more now.

When I lifted my arms, he peeled my dress over my head, and I unbuttoned his pants. I couldn't get his clothes off fast enough.

His eyes scoured my body, and his hands pressed at my waist. Then, he tenderly flattened his hard body against mine.

Lips on lips, fingers laced together, his chest against my chest.

Lightly, he skimmed my hips and eased my legs apart, and a whimper escaped me. I cradled him between my knees, and when I felt his hard length at my center, I bit my lip at the sensations coursing through my body, my nerves tingling.

I quivered as a slew of emotions passed through me—nervousness, excitement, impatience. But, when I stared into his eyes that melted my insides like chocolate sitting out in the sun, all the nervousness dissipated.

I wanted this. I wanted him.

After slipping on a condom, he entered me and I pulled at his neck until he met my lips. His movements were slow and deliberate at first but increased in pace.

"You feel so good," he groaned.

My thoughts were fragmented, my voice gone, as my breathing became labored.

The turbulence of desire swirling around us had my body rippling with liquid fire. When the buildup was too much, I abandoned myself to the hot tide of passion ripping through me. His eyes found mine, and I knew he was ready. He drove into me one last time, and we were both hurtled to the stars, flying in total ecstasy.

My heart beat wildly against my chest. We waited until our breathing stabilized, and our pulses returned to a normal rate. I reveled in the silence as I basked in the warmth of his body and the love that bloomed in my chest.

After he lifted his head, he brushed his nose against mine.

"Hey," he said as my eyes went half closed.

"Hey," I replied, sleepy and fully satisfied.

"I've got a question to ask you." His thumb caressed my cheek.

"Hmm?"

"What are you doing for the next eighty years?"

I laughed. "Why?"

"You know, because I just want to hang out," he said sweetly. "If that's okay."

I lifted my head and kissed his lips. "That's more than okay."

Happiness exuded from his pores, his elation uncontainable.

He grinned, lighting up the room even though it was dark outside, and then his lips met mine again in a soul-crushing kiss that I felt from the top of my scalp to my little pinkie toes.

Josh's love hadn't been fast and furious and fizzling. It had been slow-moving, creeping in when I hadn't expected it, infiltrating every part of my being and melting into my soul.

And I knew this love . . . our love wasn't fleeting. This was permanently real.

THE NEXT FEW MONTHS FLEW by in a blur, as if being with Josh had placed my life on fast-forward.

Every day was new and exciting. We experienced new restaurants weekly and walked at the park almost every day. Even the simple things, like sitting at a café while I read a book and he studied, were exciting. The comfort of his arms held me every night while he listened to me complain about my stressful days at work. We laughed together all the time and couldn't get enough of each other.

I realized that I'd missed the stability of being in a relationship. My last real relationship in college seemed like eons ago.

With Josh, being in love was effortless, as easy as taking in my next breath.

I stood in the middle of my living room, waiting for Josh's surprise.

"Are your eyes closed?" he asked.

"Why?" I crossed my arms over my chest and rolled to my tippy-toes and back down, digging my heels into the living room floor.

"Because." He laughed. "Just shut your eyes, Princess."

I tightly shut my eyes, and then a big thud made me jump. Something was pushing up against my foot. "What is this?"

"Don't. Open. Your eyes."

I pushed out my lip and placed my hands on my hips. "You're being kind of mean and bossy. I'm not sure I like your alter ego."

"You didn't mind my bossiness last night." There was an underlying seductiveness in his voice. He placed one hand on my hip, his fingertips caressing my side, blazing a trail of fire as they went.

My breath hitched when he pulled me against him.

"You want me to stop being bossy? You don't like the alpha in this male?"

I laughed as his hot breath formed goose bumps against my neck. "Can I please open my eyes?"

He swiftly pecked me, and automatically, I leaned in, wanting more.

"Sure."

When I opened my eyes, I blinked down at the large box wrapped in duct tape. I narrowed my eyes and tapped the box. "Really?" I complained.

He shrugged. "You'd better start. It was a bitch to wrap, so I'm assuming it'll take you some time to open." The glint of amusement brightened his face.

I dropped to my knees and started to peel off the gray industrial tape. Piece by annoying piece. "You don't mess around."

He chuckled before sitting Indian-style next to me, drumming his fingers on the floor.

"What is this for anyway? It's not my birthday."

"Can't I get you a just-because gift?" He pecked my lips and backed away as quickly as he'd come.

"What's up with you and your weekly just-because gifts?"

My man spoiled me rotten with flowers, chocolates, and stuffed animals. He'd hide the gifts in random places, just like he'd hidden his notes months ago.

He touched the tip of my nose. "Because I love you."

Le sigh.

My heartbeat quickened each time he uttered those words.

Every time he said the L-word, a cheesy smile would adorn my face, and my insides would melt like chocolate flowing from a fondue fountain.

He poked my side, and I jumped. "Hurry up. I have an exam to study for."

I saluted, and my hands worked double time, stripping each piece of tape from the box. Just when I thought I was done, I wasn't.

I pouted when red duct tape appeared under the gray. "You're so mean."

"Keep going, Princess." He fake yawned, stretching his hands to the ceiling. He lay down on the floor, one arm propping his head up.

Two dimples flashed my way—my favorite two dimples that made my heart go bumpety-bump-bump.

"Horrible. Mean. Boyfriend."

He simply grinned.

Then, I saw it—the gleam of my KitchenAid. But not my old, rusty one that they didn't even sell the replacement parts for anymore. No, this one was shiny, new, and bright red. The one I had always wanted and drooled over at the department store.

"Josh," I breathed as I pulled at the tape, seeing the picture on the box. "Josh!" I peered up to meet his eyes. "This is more than a just-because gift. It's a birthday, anniversary, and next birthday gift!"

I knew how much an industrial KitchenAid cost, and it wasn't cheap. *How could he afford this by selling shoes?* Josh's grandfather had made sure that any access to Stanton money was denied. Not that Josh would take money with stipulations.

I wanted to hug the box and jump up and down, but I was worried about his finances. "Josh, you can't afford this."

He shook his head. "Stop. I work."

I blew out a breath. "No."

"Why not?" He sat up, reached for my hand and pulled me onto his lap. "A simple thank-you will do."

I took his face in my hands, fiercely kissing him on the lips. I was so grateful for his selfless nature, but this was too much. "Maybe when you're a big, bad child services lawyer."

He nuzzled his nose against my cheek. The mere touch of his skin against mine sent a warm shiver through my body.

"I doubt I'll be rich and famous by then. I'll be working pro bono mostly. But it doesn't matter. I'll get us by." He tenderly kissed the corner of my mouth.

I peered into his eyes that held such adoration, such love. The way he'd said *us*, the confidence in that word, widened my smile.

"Accept it." He tucked some loose strands of my hair behind my ear. "It's selfish really. You'll save time, so you can bake me more brownies and cookies. What do you say?" He pushed out his bottom lip in the cutest pout. "Please."

I took in his boyish face, his warm brown eyes, and his nonstop selflessness. "Thank you, baby." I kissed his cheek and then his lips. "Thank you so much." *For everything* did not need to be said.

I stood and pulled him to his feet. "So, what's the plan tonight?"

He wrapped his arms around my waist as I admired the new box, eager to open it.

"I was thinking, maybe you could cook my just-because-I-love-you dinner?" He flashed his sexy dimple, the one that melted my insides and made me swoon.

"For sure." I buried my hands through his thick hair and pulled him in at the nape of his neck. After a chaste kiss, I pushed him toward my couch in the living room. "Go relax, my mighty shoe salesman, and study your heart out. I'll be slaving over your frozen pizza in my kitchen." I winked.

He kissed my cheek. "I've hit the jackpot. Jack. Pot!"

I watched his sexy ass swagger over and sit down on the couch, his oversize book in his hands.

I didn't really cook Josh a frozen pizza. He deserved the finest steak, but I only had burgers in our fridge, so that was what I served an hour later.

We were seated at the kitchen table when Chloe walked in, her sharp suit wrinkled after a day's work.

"Hey." After an awkward wave, she strolled into her bedroom and emerged in jeans and a T-shirt. "Hey," she said again with another weird wave.

"Hey, Chloe." Josh's head ducked toward his book, as he continued to chomp on his burger. He hadn't noticed Chloe's weird behavior.

Thing was, I knew Chloe like the lines on the inside of my palm. She was upset about something.

I frowned. "What's wrong?"

She shifted her weight, fidgeting with the edge of her shirt. "Nothing." She plopped on a chair opposite Josh and right next to me.

"Do you want a burger?" I tipped my head back to the stove. "I put one in the pan for you."

She shook her head and blew out a long breath. "So, have you turned on the television lately?" she asked, her tone cautious.

Josh's head popped up mid bite. "She's been cooking, and I've been studying all day."

The air was sucked out of the room, like a vacuum sealing a bag.

Chloe and Josh shared a knowing look. One that was understood without words.

I knew something big had hit the wall, and it probably had to do with a certain rock star.

"What happened?" Anxiety bubbled up my throat. I didn't want to know, but I did.

Chloe bit her lip and wrung her hands together on the table, her fingers turning a light pink.

"Oh, for Christ's sake." I stood and stalked into the living room, toward our coffee table. I grabbed the remote and turned on the television before dropping the remote back onto the table.

"No!" Chloe said.

But she was too late.

My hand flew to my heart as I watched the newscaster say, "Dana Calvin, the mother of Def Deception's Hawke Calvin, died today, losing her battle with cancer."

The picture that flashed on the screen was of Hawke in front of the hospital, sitting on the sidewalk. His hands were covering his face. He clearly looked emotional and broken as millions of photographers snapped their pictures around him. Near a limo, Cofi was standing only a few feet away from where Hawke was mourning.

I knew Hawke was at his weakest moment because he hated the Satan Posse, and if they were witnessing his suffering, that only meant, for once, he was unconcerned about them watching him.

The reporter continued, "Hawke Calvin was there during her final hours. Our hearts go out to him during this time."

Then, the screen flashed to a picture during Hawke and his mom's happier days. Hawke must have been around twelve or thirteen. His mom had ducked close to his face and taken a picture.

"Dana's push and marketing of a group of young boys from Madison, Wisconsin led to their success, playing in sold-out stadiums worldwide. Hawke shocked his fans when he emancipated himself from his mother at a young age of sixteen. Her addiction . . ."

The TV shut off.

When I turned, Josh was holding the remote, a guarded look in his eyes. I blinked up at him, unmoving, as my stomach churned with anxiety.

Chloe rushed toward me and gathered me in her arms. "I know it must be hard, seeing him like that, but he's going to be fine. He's going to be fine."

Josh studied me, unsure of what he should do, probably wondering what I would do next. I wasn't sure myself.

Even though we weren't together, I hurt for Hawke. I could feel his pain.

The picture of Hawke cowering into himself would forever be embedded in my brain.

My hand flew to my chest as memories of my own mother's death rushed to the surface. I had held her lifeless hand within mine, crying tears that would not stop.

I sat down on the couch for the next few minutes, just quietly letting my thoughts race, while Josh cleaned up the kitchen. My face stayed even for his benefit. I had done my best with not letting my emotions show. I knew Josh was worried about me, probably curious why I cared so much about a guy I was no longer involved with. But, as much as I wanted to deny it, I was still emotionally attached to Hawke.

I tried to stop thinking of Hawke's mother and the hurt he must be feeling right now. I tried not to think of Hawke and the way he was suffering. But, most of all, I tried not to think of his upward battle with the same type of addiction his mother had fought before cancer had taken her life.

Deep down, I hoped he would beat the system.

Deep down, I prayed that he already had.

chapter NINE

JOSH SAT AT THE EDGE of the bed and watched me from the corner of his eye. I opened my dresser to change, and the first thing my fingers reached for was a Def Deception T-shirt, faded over the years. It was my usual go-to at-home T-shirt, but I had stopped wearing it after Hawke and I had stopped talking.

Pushing it aside, I reached for another shirt with an animated panda on it and slipped on some shorts.

After I climbed into bed, Josh pulled me into his arms. I wanted to feel the comfort of his hold, the tenderness of his touch, the love in his voice, but it was wrong. Wrong to have him comfort me about a man he despised.

"It's okay to grieve, to feel sad. And to even wonder how . . . Hawke is doing."

I noticed the hesitation in his sentence, the drop in his tone as he'd said, "Hawke."

An awkwardness filled the room, which was not typical in our relationship.

I pulled his arms around me tighter. "Just hold me, please." I needed the warmth back into my body, life into my next breath.

And he did.

Because he always did.

He held me until he fell asleep. I closed my eyes and tried to clear my mind, hoping the rise and fall of Josh's chest against mine would lull me to sleep, but when my eyes shut, I pictured Hawke, alone and in pain and suffering over his mother's death.

My cell rang against the nightstand, and I blinked, staring, not moving. My heart rate picked up, and I threw my legs over my bed, slipped on my slippers, and walked over to the other side of the room.

"Hello?" My voice was whisper-soft, barely audible.

There was no way.

No way.

No way it could be him.

"Sunshine?"

It was him.

My name fell from his lips in a sore sigh. There was an ache in his voice, and I hurt for him, but I immediately realized his voice did nothing to my heart.

No pitter-patter. No shortness of breath. No irregular heartbeats.

I was over him.

All I felt was loss. Loss for him and a familiar ache caused by pain from death that was now shared between us. We'd both lost our mothers.

"Sunshine."

He sounded like he was crying, and my insides churned.

I gripped the phone tighter against my ear. "Hi," I croaked out, sympathy leaking in my tone.

When Josh shifted in my bed, I went into the bathroom and shut the door behind me.

"She's dead," he said with such a woeful finality that heat formed behind my eyes.

A jagged breath escaped him, hoarse, rough, and raspy. "I can't leave my hotel. It's crazy outside. And, right now, I can't deal."

I bit my lip and played with the edge of my shorts, swallowing a lump the size of a baseball in the back of my throat. "Were you with her?"

A desolate cry broke from his lips that sent razor blades to slice open my chest.

"I'll tell you everything. She's dead, Sunshine. She's dead."

That word brought me back to years ago when my mother had died.

"Dead," the doctor had said.

"Dead," Chloe had consoled.

"Dead," the pastor had uttered.

"I . . . I feel so alone. I am alone. When I close my eyes, I see her lifeless on that fucking hospital bed. All I hear is the breathing machine and the heart monitor flatlining. I can't fucking take it, Sunshine." He released a soft cry, like the sound of an animal in pain, one that would not come from a male of his stature.

My breathing slowed, and I tried to stop the upheaval of emotions coursing through me. An internal battle began. A part of me needed to console him, but another part of me—Chloe's voice—told me it wasn't my problem to deal with. My thoughts flickered to my boyfriend lying quietly in my bed.

"I'm with Josh now," I said.

Hawke should know that I'd moved on, that my heart belonged to someone else, that I was in love with someone else.

There was silence on the other line for several long seconds, and I heard him inhaling and exhaling.

"I only want to talk," he said, his voice shaking with a desperation that made my muscles tense. "That's it. Please."

The misery in his tone was palpable, vivid, as though I could picture him, all alone, in a dark hotel room, cowered over and crying. The visual in my mind broke me down.

When I didn't say anything for a moment, I heard a strangled sob escape him.

"I didn't know if I should believe her until . . . until it was too late, and we were both trying to make up for lost time."

The cry of this broken man slashed my insides, like paper through a shredder.

"Please. I need you. I don't talk to anybody else, and I don't want to turn to anything else."

I could feel Hawke teetering on the brink of utter destruction.

His vices. He was talking about his addiction.

He was choosing me over his addiction. He was reaching out for help.

And then, suddenly, that tiny space in my heart, the one he'd once occupied, opened.

"I just want this to end. All of it. This hurt. This pain. The guilt. I just want to talk. I haven't touched shit in months, and . . . right now, I want to numb it all. To forget."

My eyes fell shut, and anxiety stirred within me, an anxiety caused from the fear of what could happen. And the fear of Josh. How Josh would think and feel and react. But death brought on a misery that you wanted to forget. Of all people, I understood that. If anyone, I knew what could happen to Hawke. I knew how much worse he could get.

"Okay," I finally whispered. Because I couldn't deny him someone to talk to, and if I was it, I had to be there for him. Most of all, I couldn't have his desperation turn him to using.

"Tonight? Promise me, Sunshine," he asked, pleading.

"I promise." Because time mattered. Every second counted when you were dealing with an addict.

"I'll send the car. I'm not in Chicago but close."

"Okay."

And then he hung up.

With my hands planted against the sink, I took deep breaths to calm myself because my mind was a jumbled mess. Visions of my mother in her sullen state flashed behind my eyes. The desperation in Hawke's voice and the wretchedness in his sobs were so familiar.

After I brushed my teeth and combed out my hair, I slowly opened the door and tiptoed into the room to find Josh awake, sitting on the side of the bed. The clock on my nightstand flashed red at twelve forty-seven.

He glanced down at the phone in my hands and back to my face. His eyes were hard, tight, and wary because he knew. He knew it was Hawke who had called. Maybe he also knew that it was only a matter of time before Hawke would reach out.

"He's in town again. And you're going to see him." There was no hesitation in his words, no lightness in his tone, no cheerfulness in his eyes.

When I nodded to confirm, he tore his gaze from mine, lightning fast, as if I'd just slapped him hard on the face. The muscles in his forearms bulged, and his hands gripped the edge of the mattress.

"It would have been better if someone had fucking punched me in the face a hundred times." He peered up, torment clouding his vision. One hand fisted against his chest. "Because . . ." His voice came out in sharp, broken puffs. "Shit." He blew out a long breath. "Because I guarantee you . . . it would hurt less than this."

I didn't want to hurt Josh. I loved him above Hawke, above anybody, above anything. I needed him to understand where I was coming from.

"Josh . . . he was crying. He's in the worst possible place right now," I pressed and pleaded and reasoned. "He just wants to talk as friends."

Josh didn't understand, but I did. I'd lived my life watching my mother break down with her vices until she took her own life. "He doesn't have anyone to talk to about this," I begged. "He's hurting, and he doesn't want to turn to drugs. You know me. You know what I've been through with my mother. Josh, you don't understand addiction like I do. He's suffering."

He stood and faced me, fists at his sides. "What about me?" He pounded his chest. "Shit, every time he calls, you jump." He hit his chest. "How do you think that makes me feel when I love you?"

"We are just friends." My heart was troubled and torn, hurting for Josh and the fact that I was the cause of his pain. "I don't love him. I love you," I uttered the words with fierce passion because it was the truth.

He gritted his teeth, fury rising up on his face. "He's hurting? I'm fucking hurting, okay? Every time you go see him, I can't take it, Sam. I can't. Every second, I'll be going fucking crazy." His eyes widened, and his temper flared. "I. Need. You."

He walked toward me and reached for my hand, his eyes building with pure desperation. "I need you to stay here with me. I need you to forget about him. He's your past, and I want to be your future. I need you to keep him in your past, Sam. For me. Please."

My lips quivered with emotion, and I blinked back tears, torn in half—not my heart because my heart wholly belonged to Josh, but my mind. My mind was conflicted between what I wanted to do and what I should do. Josh was my future, and I wanted to stay with Josh, but I couldn't ignore this.

The echoes of Hawke's cries were still resonating in my ears.

"A grown man is crying out for help." I brushed tears out of my eyes as all my feelings bubbled to the surface. "What do you want me to do? Just turn around and pretend it's not happening?"

"Yes. That's exactly what I expect you to do, Sam."

The air released in my lungs in one large swoop, like a balloon popped by a pin.

His jaw locked, and we engaged in a silent fight. I realized where he stood, but I couldn't just walk away.

And, after a few seconds of silence, he knew I had made up my mind.

He ripped his gaze from mine and stared blankly at the wall. "I can't keep doing this." He furrowed his brow, "I can never compete with a rock star, Sam. As hard as I try, as much as I love you, I'll never win."

"But you don't have to compete," I begged, reaching for him, needing the warmth of his touch, needing him to believe me. "You've already won. I choose you. I. Choose. You."

When he tore away from my grasp, more tears burst through.

"It doesn't feel that way." When he faced me, his eyes were resolute. "Are you going to see him?"

I bit my tongue hard enough to taste blood, afraid to answer, afraid to reveal my decision.

"I've never given you an ultimatum, Sam. I don't believe in them."

Of course he didn't because his grandfather had pulled that card.

"Don't start then." I bit my cheek to control the emotions running through my veins.

In the span of the brown eyes looking straight at me, I knew that Josh occupied a piece of my heart, a permanent one, but I still couldn't ignore the pull to Hawke, the hopelessness in his voice, and his cries for help.

And Josh knew it. He could read it in my eyes.

"Sam? Are you going to see him?" His eyes twinkled with anger. He wanted to hear me say it out loud.

Pictures of my mother lying motionless on her bed pushed to the surface. I didn't want a repeat. I couldn't have a repeat of something I could control.

With one nod of my head, he picked up his pants from the floor. "Fuck this!"

"Josh, don't!" My hand stretched out to reach for him, tears flowing from my eyes in an endless stream.

He started gathering his belongings and shot past me but not before he said, "Good luck with your life, Sam. I hope you're damn happy."

"No, please!" I grabbed ahold of his arm with both hands, begging him to stay, but he shrugged me off. "Please. Please. Please."

"I'm done."

"Don't say that. Don't do this. Give me two hours."

He shook his head one last time, not bothering to turn around, and then he shut the front door behind himself.

I opened the door and followed him down the hall to the elevators. "Please, Josh. Don't do this!"

Trailing behind him, I pressed both hands against my chest, feeling my world crumbling below my feet in a never-ending pit. The elevator pinged open, and desperation shook every one of my limbs.

"Please, Josh. I. Love. You."

My words stilled him. With one hand on the elevator door, he turned around, giving me one last look, his eyes glossed over. "Then, don't go."

There it was.

The ultimatum had been laid out.

Clear as a boom of fireworks.

A stream of tears fell down each of my cheeks.

I didn't want to go, but it was like I was at the end of a suicide line. For a long time after my mother's death, I'd blamed myself, and I didn't want another repeat. I didn't want to be that person, wishing and wondering if I could have done something different, something better, something to change the outcome of what had happened. There was no way I could walk away from Hawke. Every part of me knew it would be wrong.

Josh's gaze dropped to the floor before he backed into the elevator. "Bye, Sam," he uttered, before the doors shut him in.

A rush of air escaped me, forcing me to my knees. I stared at the ground, my tears blurring my vision.

Josh.

How could I have let Josh just leave like that? I should've chased him down. I should have chased him outside.

I walked back into my apartment in a daze, heaving in and out, heart palpitating in a full-blown panic attack.

Josh had to know I loved him. He just didn't understand. He didn't get how addiction worked. He hadn't been there when my mother died, so although he could empathize, he wouldn't really know. I needed more time to convince him to see my side of things. But time was something I didn't have.

I'd convince him later. I'd make him see. Make him understand. Make him forgive me.

The ringing on my phone brought me out of my thoughts. When I picked up on the third ring, it was Tilton.

"Miss Clarke, I'm downstairs."

I nodded and blew out a breath.

I needed a clear state of mind to help Hawke.

Breathe. Breathe. Breathe.

I closed my eyes and pulled myself together, knowing the best way to handle this situation was to tackle things one at a time. "I'll be down in five."

Once in the stretch limo, I tried to prod Tilton with questions, but his one-worded answers told me nothing. Our ride took less than thirty minutes. We ended up in Schaumburg, a suburb north of Chicago. The Hyatt Hotel sign shone brightly against the dark night sky.

"Why is he here?"

"He flew here straight after his mother's death. To see you, Miss Clarke."

I swallowed back a lump in my throat. Of course he had. Tilton's words solidified my decision to come. Josh just didn't understand. He was angry at a decision I *had* to make.

He doesn't understand, but I'll make him, I repeated to myself.

"He's not good. Not good at all," Tilton confirmed.

My stomach churned into a triple knot, one that you couldn't untie.

Tilton's usual response of, "He's well," was not present.

Tilton led me into the hotel and through a back entrance. I'd been this way before, just at a different hotel, at a different time, and under a different circumstance.

When I entered the massive penthouse, Tilton shut the door

behind me. The air around me chilled me to the bone, and the only sound that I could hear was the blowing of the heater in the background. The space was untouched, super clean, like no one occupied the room.

I padded across the living room floor and turned on all the lights. Still, no Hawke in sight, but the dull, lifeless aura in the atmosphere had me brokenhearted. I opened the door to his bedroom and found him sitting at the edge of the bed, beer in hand, hair a disheveled mess.

His red-rimmed eyes glanced up to me with a despair I'd once been familiar with.

"Sunshine . . ."

The way he'd said my name, as though I were the sun shining down into the pits of wretched misery, rammed directly in my chest and had me determined to get him out of his depressed state.

I sat next to him on the bed and extended a consoling hand. "I'm sorry, Hawke."

He peered down to where our hands were joined. "I didn't think you would come." The words were thick with emotion, husky with anguish.

"I promised, didn't I?" I squeezed his hand, letting him know I was physically here, that when I promised, I meant it.

"Yeah, but things are different now." His sullen tone increased, and his head dropped to the ground, a man already defeated.

I squeezed his hand tighter and ducked my head to get into his line of sight, emphasizing my words as I said, "I'll always be your friend, Hawke."

And I would be. He didn't have many, given his lifestyle, and I knew the value of a good friend. I had that in Chloe.

He nodded and then a heavyhearted sob escaped him, the same hopeless one I'd heard on the phone. "I didn't believe her." He released me and turned away, not wanting me to see his tears. "She said she was trying to get clean before the cancer hit. That was months before I decided to get clean myself."

I sagged against the bed, relief flooding my insides.

He was clean and off drugs, and I knew me coming here wasn't all in vain.

"I hired an addiction counselor," he said quietly. "We took her on tour, and she kept us off everything." He scratched at his brow and then gripped the top of his head.

I'd had no idea. I had purposely stayed off social media and stopped watching the news to avoid seeing him.

"My mother couldn't fight the battle until it was too late." He covered his eyes with one hand, his breaths shallow, his shoulders hunched. "I know all the things I said about her before, but . . . she was my mom. Yeah, we didn't agree, but she backed us up and pushed us to rise to fame when we were fifteen. We saw what money could buy, what it could do, and she drilled it into my head that we would never let it overtake us. We always had to make sure it was about the music." He paused, sucking in a breath. "It used to be all about the music."

With one hand, I rubbed his back, trying to console him.

He took a shaky breath. It was as though it hurt him to talk, hurt to breathe, hurt to reminisce about a past with his mother. "Then, it consumed her. The money. The fame. She was tired all the time, worn down, and she needed the coke to maintain the high."

He swallowed back his tears, turning to bury his face in my skin. When his warm, wet tears touched my neck, the heartache in my chest intensified, and I had to fight off my own tears. I'd never seen him so vulnerable.

"Then, I got so fucking mad at her." His voice was barely audible, and I strained to hear him. "She'd schedule two interviews at the same time. Overpromise us when we were already committed. We fought constantly, and I told her we needed to slow down. We led this. Without us, there was no band, no fame, no money, but she kept pushing and pushing until, eventually, I had enough."

I hugged him tighter, wanting to consume some of his pain. His tears, his sorrow, his anguish caused me to tremble.

"That's what power and fame will do to you." His tone was low, defeated. "You don't want the high to ever stop because you're afraid it'll disappear. You'll be forgotten. I get it, but that was never going to happen. I would never let us die.

"When I was at the hospital, she apologized. She was so weak, but she said she loved me, and she was sorry for what she'd put me through. She's the only family I've ever had. The one in the beginning who started us up. I wouldn't be here if it wasn't for her, the band wouldn't be here . . . and now, she's gone."

When his body racked with soft sobs, I couldn't control my emotions any longer, and a hot tear rolled down my cheek. He cowered into me, reminding me of a lost, broken boy desperately looking for his mother, needing her.

"She was tired and ready, but I still begged her not to go. I wished I had gotten there sooner, that I'd believed her. Because all of this—the fame, the money—it doesn't seem to matter anymore." He shook his head in a continuous motion, as though he still couldn't believe it, couldn't grasp the idea that she was gone.

"It's not your fault," I told him as tears coursed down my own face, my lip quivering with emotion. "After all the lies she fed you through the years, how were you supposed to know she was telling the truth this time?"

Those same words had been said to me over and over again—by my counselor, by Chloe's parents, by Chloe.

"I've been here, Hawke. I know how you're feeling. My mother battled addiction with opiates and painkillers for years." More tears pushed through as my breathing slowed, and my heart constricted with the memory. "I always wondered how I could have done things differently . . . changed the outcome of what had happened."

A strangled sob escaped me, but I pushed through. "Know that you did all that you could, given the circumstances. She loved you, and now . . . she's in a better place. She's no longer hurting. But I promise . . . I promise you, Hawke . . . this will get easier."

It was only after the storm when I'd realized rays of sunshine were coming through the clouds. Hawke couldn't see that now. It was too soon. It might take years, but he would see it eventually.

His arms fell against my waist, and he hugged me into him, breathing me in, and I let him. I understood the pain of losing someone so close that it physically hurt you. Like the emotion hurt from the inside out.

"It's okay," I whispered over and over again, heat forming behind my eyes. "It's fresh, but your mom loved you, and she knows you loved her, too." It tortured me to see a grown man crying so inconsolably.

"I don't know what I'd do without you, Sunshine. I love you, baby . . . so much."

A shiver ran through his body, but mine stayed utterly still. The words he'd uttered did nothing to my heart anymore. It was his tears that seared through me.

"I hate myself. It should have been me, not her."

Warning bells rang loudly in my head, like a fire alarm in a burning building, and I knew the negative thoughts had to stop. They would only lead to bigger issues.

I threaded my fingers together at the base of his neck. "Don't say that."

His sorrow brought back all my pent-up hopelessness. There was a time when I'd wished it had been me instead. The pain had been so unbearable, I didn't know how to function. Flashes of my mother ran through my brain like a flip book, stills of her perfect face moving in slow motion. Her laughter, her tears, her joys that had filled my days with happiness.

And that happiness had turned into inconsolable heartbreak.

Her sadness . . . the despair she'd felt toward the end. The cheerless person I no longer knew until it was too much for her to take.

Tears sprang to my eyes. "I know how you feel, Hawke. I do. Above anyone else, I know how you feel, and I promise, it'll get better. She might not be here now, but you just have to believe that it will get better. Hold on to the last time you saw her, you held her hands, and be thankful she knew you loved her. Wherever she is, she knows she was loved. She was here, she was loved by you, and she wasn't alone when she died."

The dam opened, and tears continued to flow as the emotions deep inside me were laid out for him to see. His arms clutched on to me, as though I were his lifeline, and then we collapsed into each other, using one another for support.

"I loved her. I kept telling her every single day. Every single hour. That she was loved," he said brokenly.

Then, he pulled back and kissed me, so abruptly that I didn't have a chance to stop him.

"We can't," I said, tearing my lips away from him. "I love Josh."

I hadn't come to Hawke to get back with him. I'd only come to console him.

"We can't do this," I said, our tears meshing together in a stream of heavyhearted sorrow.

He ignored me and kissed me again with such fervor, a kiss so heavy with misery, that it took me with him.

"I feel numb. All of me," he breathed. His fingers gripped my waist, desperately pulling me into him. "Take my pain away. I need to feel, and I only feel alive when I'm with you."

One second.

One breath.

No exhale.

"Hawke . . ."

His hands went to the button of my jeans.

His tears. My tears.
His hands. My hands.
His clothes. My clothes.
We met where passion forgot pain.

chapter **TEN**

IT WAS OVER AS FAST as it'd started. Hawke on top of me, me cradling him between my legs, ending with me in his arms. He pulled me into him, spooning me from behind. His tears had ceased, but mine continued. But harder and for a different reason—guilt.

I could've stopped him. I had a voice. I could have said no, but he was in pain with an ache so strong, something that I understood. And he had said I was the only girl he'd ever loved, the only person who mattered. Through his deep-rooted miserable sobs, I had wanted to console him, ease his anguish, and I'd wanted to ease mine, but we'd taken it too far.

They said it took one moment, a split second, to make a decision that could change the rest of your life, and I knew I had made mine. The instant I'd let Hawke take me I knew that my future—the one I had hoped to have with Josh—was over.

My cries turned into sobs, and sobs turned into hiccups. I knew Hawke was asleep from his soft breaths against my neck. In that moment, I hated myself. For betraying Josh, for not fighting hard enough for the both of us. I hated that one second that I could've taken another route, and I hadn't.

I glanced over at Hawke. His face was still beautifully perfect, just as it was pictured on every poster or best-selling magazine adorning the walls of millions of women. But it was no longer what I wanted.

He'd said he loved me, but the fairy tale of me and the rock star, married with kids and on tour, in a mansion, was not something I longed for.

In that brief moment of passion, I had felt nothing.

A constant knock on the door forced me to sit up on the bed. My breathing slowed as I slipped out of bed, walked out of the bedroom, and down the foyer to open the door. My eyes took in the sexy brunette in a fitted black halter-top dress.

She walked straight past me.

"Hey!"

I tried to stop her, but she strolled toward Hawke's bedroom, ignoring the fact that the thin fabric of the sheet was covering my naked body, ignoring me completely.

She knows where his bedroom is. She's been here.

"Excuse me. Who are you? What are you doing here?"

She approached his bed, dropped on all fours, and reached for something under the bed. After pulling out a small black purse, she stood and flattened her hands down her dress. She peered at Hawke soundly sleeping on his stomach, ass cheeks on display.

"I have to admit, he's a fucking fine specimen. Not to mention, great in bed."

Her words were like a sledgehammer slamming against my skull, causing me to stagger back.

"Don't look at me like that." Her tone was suave and smooth, matching her demeanor. "Let me guess. You met him at a concert." She paused, waiting for me to confirm, to heighten the blow when she already knew. "Now, you're special. You mean something to him, right?" She let out a low laugh and slipped her bag over her shoulder. "We're not special. I was here to help him forget today. I'm sure you were here to do the same thing." She tipped her head in my direction. "The difference between you and me is that I get paid, and I'm good at what I do."

I held my stomach, feeling unsteady. I had no words, and I doubted my ability to speak.

My facial features fell because I couldn't hold up my poker face any longer, and then I saw it—pity. I read the pity in her eyes. And I knew why. She had come here, fully knowing what the real deal was, where I had been played—played like a sad song.

"Just telling you how it is. It'll save *you* girls a lot of heartbreak later. My company's very discreet and tight-lipped about all our clients. That's why he's been a client of ours for years. I mean, it's my first time with him, but I've seen his file."

My body visibly shook, every one of my muscles trembled. Bile formed behind my throat.

"He never wants the same girl. He wants a different girl every few weeks. Just like clockwork." She walked past me, her words fleeting and without malice, which made the hurt in my arms, in my head, in my chest worse.

I didn't have time to see her walk out before I ran to the bathroom, dropped to the floor and dry-heaved over the toilet as hot tears streamed down my face. Nothing was coming out. I stuck my finger down my throat to throw up because, sometimes, throwing up when I felt sick to my core made me better. But nothing was coming out when I wanted everything to come out—the dirt, the guilt, my endless believing heart.

The satin sheet lay below my feet as memories of our months together flew past me like a bad dream. I'd wanted to believe him, so I had. The heart and mind had wanted to believe what they wanted to believe, giving into his tales to be happy, but that happiness had been fake because that happiness had been built on lies.

I stood, needing to get out of this place. After rushing to the bedroom, I staggered mid step, seeing him sleeping on the bed. I slipped on my clothes, and another rush of unease filled my belly. My hands cupped my mouth as I rushed to the bathroom . . . again.

I needed something, anything, to curb this foul taste in my mouth. I pulled open the drawers, looking for toothpaste or mouthwash, *something*. But then the tears ceased, and my stomach dropped and kept going. Or maybe it was my heart. Who knew?

But I heard the crack when it tumbled onto the marble.

Two quarter-sized plastic bags with white powder sat next to a vial with multiple needles. Prescription drugs were laid out in the drawer.

The lies were endless, the deceit infinite.

My pulse skyrocketed. I'd never experienced a full-on panic attack, but I was sure that was what I was going through now.

My vision blurred, and the next thing I knew, I was frantically searching through Hawke's suitcases in his bedroom. Underneath his clothes were more of the same things—packets of white powder, vials of liquid, and needles. A ton of needles. And condoms, enough to screw an army of groupies, which I was sure he'd done.

My body temperature elevated, and hot sweats flushed every millimeter of my skin.

My jaw clenched. The muscles in my neck tensed, sweat forming at my brow. Manic deep breaths shook me. I was going to be sick. Again.

This time, I swallowed back the bile that crept up my throat and forced my feet to steady.

Stupid. Stupid. Stupid girl!

I wanted to pull my hair out. I was so stupid.

In the next second, I didn't think. I just reacted. My hands moved of their own accord, and I scooped up all his shit and rushed to the bathroom. It looked like I was the head of a drug cartel as I laid everything at my feet. Then, I began to get rid of everything, emptying the powder and the prescription drugs and vials into the toilet and flushing. Like I was a madwoman, I was just dumping and flushing, dumping and flushing.

There was probably over a hundred thousand dollars' worth of drugs here, but it didn't matter. I was sure he'd get more.

I was on my knees, dumping the last of the drugs when he walked in. His eyes widened at the mess.

"What are you doing?" His face turned to panic as he reached for me.

I shoved at his chest, going ballistic. "You're a fucking liar! Liar!" I screamed. "I hate you. I hate you!" Tears coursed down my face, and I hated that he was seeing me cry, yet I couldn't stop the tears from falling.

He let me push him and yell, and he didn't say one thing during my tirade, which only confirmed that I was right. He was still using.

When I was done screaming, my throat burned like I'd drunk acid.

He came toward me, his eyes cautious and guilty. "Sunshine, calm down."

"Fuck you!" I backed away slowly, so he could see and feel the anger emanating from my every pore. I didn't need to tell him about his female visitor because I was done. "I don't to hear your lies anymore. I don't want anything to do with you. You are scum. You are nothing to me." I raised my chin, my eyes never leaving his.

The look on his face told me that my words had gutted him, but I kept going because he had played me for a fool. All this time.

I took in a deep breath through my nose, regaining control. "You contact me, I swear to God, I'll tell the world. I'll sell our story to the paparazzi. All of it. I'll make millions, and they'll love every word."

He took another step, his hand outstretched.

Palms up, I screamed, "Don't touch me! You don't deserve to touch me. I hate you. Do you hear me? I. Hate. You."

My eyes filled with a hatred so strong, I was shaking.

When I rushed into the bedroom, Hawke followed.

Tilton was there to greet me, probably alarmed from all the commotion.

"Sunshine . . ." Hawke called out my name.

But I blocked out his voice. I wished I could erase the sound, his tone, his everything from my memory.

I moved past Tilton to reach for my purse and shoes by the bed.

After slipping on my Converse, I rushed toward the door but not before Hawke's hard tone called out, "Tilton."

One word, and the big beast was in front of me, blocking my path to the exit. I flipped around, one hand fisted against my purse, the other tightly clenched at my side. Neck taut, eyes fuming, I dared him to stop me from leaving.

"NDA, Tilton."

It took a few moments before the acronym registered. *Nondisclosure agreement.*

I blinked a few times, unable to fathom what was happening. Who was this guy that I'd thought I knew?

I held my chin high. "I'm not signing one," I said with such force and such certainty that he had to know that blood would be shed before I signed any piece of paper. I would have no freedom from him then. If I didn't have this to hold over his head, I'd never get him to leave me alone.

I wanted nothing from him, nor did I want to be involved in his lifestyle, the glamour that was made-up fairy tales. Everything I had experienced with the rock star was laced with drugs, partying, and an endless life of shed tears. I would no longer fall for his lies, feel pity for him. He was beyond saving because he was the Devil himself. I could take control of my own life, and Hawke was no longer a part of it.

"Don't contact me. Ever," I said coolly. "Or I'll go through with my word." I glowered, my eyes conveying the fury within me. "You wouldn't know what love is. You don't know love."

"Sunshine"—his shoulders curled in over his chest, and his tone visibly shook—"don't." His eyes were begging, trying one more time.

But it was fake. And his voice no longer affected me.

I turned to leave and walked out the door, never looking back.

I made a solemn vow to myself. I would never, ever see Hawke again.

chapter ELEVEN

MY HEAD RESTED AGAINST THE headboard of my bed, feet over my comforter, as I held an opened envelope in my hand.

I got in.

Into Le Cordon Bleu.

But that wasn't what was in the forefront of my mind.

"Call him." Chloe pushed my cell toward me, but all I wanted to do was lie in my bed. Forever. "It's been weeks," she said, as if I needed reminding.

What did she want me to do? Beg for him back? I didn't deserve him. He'd never forgive me. I'd never forgive myself.

"I'm not calling him." My voice was fragile, shaky, just like my insides. "He deserves so much better than me."

She nodded. "That, he does, but I hate seeing you so miserable, and from his texts, I know he's miserable, too."

I peered up at her, my eyebrows pulling together. "You've been texting him?"

"Yes." Blunt, honest, and to the point. "And he's been texting me back."

Jealousy spiked within me. They were strictly friends, but envy filled my veins. I wanted Josh texts. Happy, silly, emoji-filled texts.

"What has he said?" I didn't want to be curious, but I wanted to know everything he had been doing. Every single thing.

I wanted him to sing horribly in my ear. I wanted him to hold me and utter his crazy, corny lines.

Heat formed behind my eyes. Just when I thought I had cried all my tears, there were more. All because of my own stupidity.

Her lips pursed together, as though she were thinking about something in her head. "He doesn't ask about you. And I know why." She angled closer, her eyes thoughtful. "It's because it hurts too much, I'm sure. I know heartbreak. It hurts. Everything hurts. Even when he hears your name, it hurts. More so when he says it." She put a consoling hand on my shoulder, her eyes firmly meeting mine. "And, if he doesn't ask about you, that doesn't mean that he's not thinking about you. In my opinion, if he's not asking about you, he's thinking about you more."

My chin dipped into my chest, guilt rising within me. "I messed up. So bad, Chloe. I go back to that one second every single day. That one nanosecond when I felt sympathy and sadness, and in that one brief moment, I fell weak."

She blew out a breath, and I knew she understood. "You're dumb and naive, and Hawke played the right cards. I'm not saying he wasn't depressed about his mother's death. I'm saying that he used your compassion, knowing you had a boyfriend, and seduced you anyway."

I shook my head, not wanting to relive one of the worst nights of my life. "Enough." I dropped my gaze to my purple comforter. "I'm not going to play the victim here. I'm an adult." It took two that night. "I'm the stupidest blonde on the planet."

After a beat, she pulled me into her. It was what I needed. The comfort of her warmth and her consoling words to relieve me, like they always did. She was my angel on earth.

"You're going to do what I told you years ago," she said softly. "You're going to get up, and you're going to live." She kissed my forehead then.

She had repeated the words she had said when my mother died. After her death, Chloe had functioned as my rock, repeating those words to me like a broken record until I finally believed it.

"Live. But not too wildly this time." She tucked an escaping strand of my hair behind my ear. "The best thing that came out of this situation is that stalker-rocker of yours is out of your life. For good."

I couldn't agree with her more. Though the anger inside me had not subsided. The more I thought of Hawke, the more the hatred within me grew. The drugs. The women. The lies. And I had believed them all.

I shook those morbid thoughts out of my head. I needed to move on before it made me sick, before I sank into a hole so deep, I'd never get out.

After Chloe pulled the blanket over our knees, she grabbed the remote. "*Sex and the City?*" she asked with her signature Chloe smile.

My shoulder bumped against hers. "Yes. Nothing a little HBO and Carrie Bradshaw can't fix."

I needed laughter and sunshine to break my mood.

I craved Josh's sunshine, but that sun had set and would never rise again.

After the third episode of *Sex and the City*, I slipped out of bed to use the bathroom. When I was on the toilet, Chloe's box of tampons on the floor caught my eye.

I blinked.

And held my breath.

Counting the days until my next cycle.

Then, it hit me.

Like a boulder against a building, taking it down and leaving destruction behind.

I was late.

Very late.

My legs shook when I stood. Then, full-body tremors took over.

"Oh, please, no," I begged, hopping on both feet.

I paced the small room, back and forth, forth and back, with no destination in mind. Then, I dropped to my knees, searching under the sink for a pregnancy test. Chloe was always safe, but for some reason, she always thought she was pregnant.

I pulled out a test from the three-pack box and waited.

Drank the sink water.

And waited some more.

Both of my hands were pressed against my head as I hovered over the sink.

When the urge came, I peed on the stick that could potentially alter my future.

I waited.

One stripe.

Then, two.

Two lines. Lines that altered my culinary career and my whole life.

I blinked, but the outcome didn't change.

In the next second, I stood, and then I crumbled to the ground. There was an intense ringing in my ears, a pain spreading to my chest, lungs, throat, and feet.

This was not happening.

Not. Happening.

How could I be so stupid? After that crazy night with Hawke, I'd gotten tested. I was clean. I hadn't contemplated being pregnant.

Who knew how much time had passed, but I stayed motionless in the same spot.

The banging on the bathroom door would not relent.

"Open up, Sammy! What the hell? A girl has to pee, too!" Chloe continued banging on the door.

The sounds of her voice and the hitting of her fist against the wood were numb in my ears. All I heard was the deep boom of my heartbeat. All I felt was the sweat on the inside of my palms. All I could see through my blinking eyes was the pink. Two stripes. Not one. On my pregnancy test.

Pregnant.

The lock of the door jiggled before she exploded into the bathroom. Her eyes dropped to me on the ground, her angry face changing a second later once she took in my reaction. Then, she glanced at the white stick I was squeezing between my fingertips. Her fist flew to her mouth. "No," she uttered.

I brought my knees up to my chest in the middle of the bathroom floor and rocked back and forth, clawing at my cheeks.

Immediately, she dropped beside me. "How late?"

I couldn't form words, let alone breathe.

"Sam." The stress was audible in her tone. "How late?"

The back of my throat felt dry, as though I had swallowed sand. "Two weeks," I whispered.

Then, she asked the question that sliced my insides.

"Do you know whose it is?"

Fresh tears formed beneath my eyelids.

The pain in the back of my throat intensified, and I cowered into myself and pressed my hand over my face. I shook my head to respond to her question.

"Oh, honey." She threw an arm over my shoulder and brought me close. "We'll get through this. I promise. Whatever you decide, we'll get through this."

The tears gushed out. I wanted to scream for release. Scream for help. Call for a time-out. Do anything but face my new reality.

She kissed my forehead. "I've got you. We've got this together."

I nodded because I needed her. Because I had to get through this. Because this wasn't about me anymore. Because it would forever include a little someone else.

BEING PREGNANT HAD BEEN A struggle at first, but I'd pushed through it. Over the next months, Chloe had been there to pull up my hair and let me throw up into the toilet. She'd cooked me anything I wanted and let me slack on the housework when my muscles were too tired to even change into my PJs after work.

Soon, the crying had stopped because I needed to take responsibility and pull up my big-girl panties. I'd realized I needed to work to save for the baby, so I'd picked up extra hours. When I wasn't working, I would be sleeping because eating was not in the baby's itinerary.

Time had flown by in a blur, and before I had known it, Chloe and I had been holding an ultrasound of our little girl, admiring the outline of her features while watching another round of *Sex and the City* in our living room. She had cried when the strong heartbeat of my baby boomed through the speakers. I swore, the doctor thought we were a couple. In a way, we were. She was my rock.

My butt was in my favorite spot, right in front of the television, as I watched my favorite show. I nudged Chloe's shoulder. "Go!"

She wasn't going to stay home to watch another round of *Sex and the City*.

"What?" She shrugged, her face telling me she wasn't moving.

"Your date, Chloe. You need to go. You can't stop your life to sit here and take care of me."

She'd been doing it for months, and her social life had taken the brunt of it.

Her eyes went back to the TV. "I choose to be here, Sam. I want to be here. I'm excited for the both of us."

I nudged her again, more forcefully this time. I could always tell when Chloe's head was turning over and over. I was sure she knew when I was working something out in my mind as well. We'd known each other long enough.

"Go! I'll be fine. Me and Baby Boo will be right here when you get back." I rubbed my baby bump, five-months prominent in my fitted shirt.

She sucked in her bottom lip, contemplating, until I stood and pulled her to stand.

I spanked her bottom. "Go! Seriously. If you don't leave, I think you'll bust from sexual frustration. It's been months since you've gotten laid."

"Earmuffs," she whispered, pointing to the baby. "Fine! But I'm only one call away. One call." She rubbed my belly before bending down to talk to the baby. "You call Auntie Chloe if you need me." She kissed my stomach before patting me on the head like I was her pet. Then, she strolled to her room.

I shook my head, amused. She'd make a wonderful mother one day—if she only wanted kids, which she didn't.

Where I wanted traditional with a quiet suburban home, Chloe was the opposite. She wanted the city life and an expensive condo on the highest floor of Chicago's tallest skyscraper. I didn't doubt her ability to achieve those dreams. Chloe worked hard to get to wherever she wanted to be. Year after year, I had seen her get promoted. It was only a matter of time before she was managing her own marketing execs.

A grumble from my stomach broke, as though the baby were talking to me. I rubbed my tiny munchkin. Little by little, the ache of raising this child alone had lessened because responsibility had stepped up and dimmed that ache. That ache had been replaced with affection and excitement of the baby to come.

"What do you want to eat?" I whispered, glad my nausea had decreased over the last few months. Slowly, my appetite had reappeared. "Did you say pizza, baby girl?" I smiled, already anticipating great food. "Have fun, Chloe," I yelled behind me before walking toward the door. "We're going for a walk and getting some pizza."

I stepped out into the cold winter night with a hat, gloves, and a coat that no longer fit because my belly was popping out.

Puffs of white air escaped my mouth when I breathed out, and I wrapped my arms around myself to keep warm. It was good to be outside and take in the fresh air. I decided, if I was going to have pizza, then it'd better be good, so I hailed a cab and told him to drive to Coozie's.

Sitting in the red cushioned seat, in the front of the store, my senses were bombarded with the spices, cheeses, and meats. I released a silent sigh when thoughts of Josh filtered through my brain. They always did, but more so now that I was having pizza at the same place where we'd argued, debating on which city served better pizza—Chicago or New York.

I took off my hat and stripped off my coat and gloves. Being pregnant, my body temperature was up and down and all around. One minute, I was freezing, and the next moment, I was hot.

I ordered a stuffed pizza with pepperoni and sausage and waited for my to-go order. I had wanted to get out and take in the fresh air, but I also wanted to eat it on the comfort of my couch.

"Sam?"

A familiar voice had me rooted in my spot.

When I peered up, the baby kicked, surprising me. My mouth slackened. My throat fell dry. I blinked rapidly, unable to process what was happening.

Many times before, I had wished for him to appear. Wishing he were still mine and this baby were his. At other times, I swore, different strangers were him, but my eyes had just been fooling me.

But, this time, it was him.

It was Josh.

Only a few feet away.

A slew of emotions passed across his face. First was a sense of longing in his eyes, and then a small smile touched his lips as he approached.

Automatically, my hands flew to my stomach—to protect the baby or myself, I didn't know.

And then his eyes dropped to where my hands had fallen. He jerked back, and his eyes went wide.

Like I had done with Hawke and all the drugs, I didn't think. I reacted.

A tiny cry escaped me, and then I tore past him, my feet hitting the pavement outside, my belly bouncing in front of me, my coat and scarf and gloves still hanging off my arm. I heard him yelling for me to stop, but I couldn't. I couldn't do anything but run. I couldn't let him see me like this. Let him know I'd been hiding this from him. Even though it might not be his.

But, Josh being Josh, he chased me down the street, through the snow, without a jacket.

With all the weight I was packing, there was no way I could outrun him.

He reached for my elbow, careful to steady me first, before he turned me to face him. His eyes searched my face before dropping to my stomach again, then returning to my face, and back and forth.

He blew out large puffs of air. With one trembling hand, he pressed his palm against my stomach. The touch was so intimate that an unexpected heat formed behind my eyes. I leaned into him, craving his touch though I didn't deserve it.

He blinked, furrowing his eyebrows. Exhaling a shaky breath, he focused on my stomach with hope and longing and love. "Is it . . . is it mine?" His voice quivered with intense emotion. He held his breath and waited, as if my one answer held his world.

A single tear fell down my cheek in slow motion, and I told him the truth that revealed everything and crushed my hope for our future. "I don't know."

In that moment, his eyes watered, clouding his vision, and he winced, as though I'd sucker-punched him in the gut with my words.

With an ache so deep in my chest, I stepped away from him for good, and his hand dropped. Then, I turned to walk away.

This time, the only time ever, he didn't follow me.

chapter TWELVE

DARKNESS SURROUNDED MY SMALL APARTMENT as I stepped inside and walked blankly to my bedroom where I slipped under the covers. The scent of leftover lasagna from the kitchen wafted toward my nose, making me feel queasy. I could eat the lasagna, but the baby wanted Coozie's, the paid pizza I'd left at the restaurant.

What happened to the stories I'd heard? About glowing and flawless skin and a happiness that filled the air to have a living human growing inside you?

Lies. All lies, so we would procreate.

But, once again, I pushed those negative thoughts aside. They were no good for the baby, and she was my priority now.

It was just so hard to be positive all the time. Especially since I'd had to decline my acceptance into Le Cordon Bleu, and I was working nonstop to save for my baby, not to mention the stress surrounding the circumstances of my pregnancy.

The doorbell buzzed, and I jumped to a sitting position, faster than a person without enough food in their stomach should. I threw my knees over the bed and went to the buzzer. I pressed the receiver and heard his familiar voice. The voice that held so much anguish.

"Sam, open up. It's me."

I closed my eyes and debated if I should let him in.

"I saw your light on," he said, determination heavy in his tone. "I know you're there. We need to talk," he pressed.

Finally, I buzzed him in and opened the door. He was standing there, in all his handsome, boyish glory, in jeans and an Illini T-shirt with his Cubs hat on and the puffy North Face bomber jacket that he had left at the restaurant before running after me.

And, in that moment, I knew I still loved him. I wanted to cry all over again for the pain I had caused, for the torment in his eyes, for my stupidity, for our lost future.

"Hi," he said, slowly stepping inside.

"Hi." Guilt ate at my core.

I was a mess inside, but I used all my energy to keep it together.

"How are you feeling?" Concern leaked from his voice.

But I didn't want his concern. I wanted his anger. Because I deserved his anger, not his concern.

It'd be better if he hated me. His kindness only made me feel worse about myself.

"I don't know why I'm here." His eyes dropped again to my stomach, and I couldn't read his face. "It's like my brain wanted me to go home, but . . . my heart had other plans." Honesty seeped out of him, which was so typical of his character. No front. No pretending he wasn't affected.

I needed him to know that I'd be okay. That he shouldn't pity me. I'd walked into this situation, and I was determined to walk out with my head held high.

"It's fine," I said, my voice fake but firm. "I'm going to be fine, and the baby is going to be fine. I'm going to do this by myself. Raise her by myself."

"Her?" He swallowed and released a breath, his face still unreadable.

I wanted to see his eyes because his eyes were the passageway to his thoughts. At one time, I could read everything he was thinking without him speaking a word.

"I'll be okay." My voice was resigned, defeated. "I wasn't going to tell you."

His face snapped up, and he let out a frustrated growl. "See, that's the problem. I have a right to know."

I looked off to the side and focused on the abstract art hanging against my white wall. I'd bought the painting at a local art fair. The array of colors had drawn me in, all blending together. You didn't know where one color ended and where the next began. The artist called it Chaos. *Story of my life.*

"Sam . . ."

He was closer now. I could feel his heat, just a foot away.

I turned toward him, and he closed the gap between us. His hands dropped to my stomach, and I froze, surprised at the contact. His eyebrows pulled together over his chocolate-brown eyes. He stared intently at my stomach where the unborn baby lay.

"Is . . . is she mine?" he asked again.

I bit my cheek hard to feel pain because my next words would be even more painful. I didn't understand why he was asking again, why he wanted to hurt all over again. He had heard me perfectly fine in front of Coozie's. The look of pain on his face would forever be embedded in my brain.

"I don't know," I repeated.

He pursed his lips and didn't step away this time as a tear escaped my eye. I didn't bother to swipe it. That would only draw attention to the fact that I was crying.

"Did you ever love me?" His eyes were still on my stomach, and he exhaled deeply, as though his life depended on that one question. "The truth now. I know you loved him, but I want to know . . . I want to know if you ever loved me."

God . . . where should I begin? I wanted to tell him I'd never been so madly in love before, how the days had blended together, and time had seemed to lapse with him. I wanted to tell him I'd made a mistake. Even though he'd broken up with me that night, in my mind, we weren't truly done. If I could take back that one night with Hawke, I would.

When I didn't answer, he cleared his throat. "God knows that I loved . . . still love you." Josh's voice shook as he spoke, his fingers trembling against my swollen stomach. "I just want to know if it was real, y'know?" His stare became distant. "Because I felt it. The way we were together. I just want to know I didn't imagine a lifetime with you just because I wanted to. That you felt it, too. That I didn't imagine it all." He clenched his jaw. "I thought we had what my parents had."

A tightness formed in the middle of my chest, making it difficult to breathe, difficult to stand, difficult to form words.

He lifted my chin to meet my eyes, his eyes glazed over. "Did you ever love me, Sam?"

I stared back at him, not wavering, and maybe I should've lied. The unselfish part of me would've, but he needed to know our relationship was real. "Yes. I loved you. So much." That last part just slipped out before another tear escaped. But it was true. I couldn't deny this love overwhelming me. My love for Josh would be forever. Every person before him was just a boy, insignificant to how I felt for him.

He released a long sigh, his tone tired. "Are you with him, Sam?"

"No, of course not."

"Do you want to be with him?"

When I didn't answer, he repeated himself, his voice gruff, "Do you?" He let out a frustrated sigh. "If you say you loved me like you did, why did you leave me that night? Why did you choose him?"

My gaze dropped to the living baby bump that was my future. I already knew my answer, and it wouldn't help. It certainly wouldn't change anything.

He threw both hands up. "Tell me."

I stayed silent because there was nothing I could say. There wasn't a reason good enough to tell him why I had left. Other than I'd thought I was doing the right thing.

"Tell me, Sam," he demanded, his hands clenching. "Damn it!"

"Because he was hurting, Josh." I wrung my hands together. Tears sprang to my eyes. "He was hurting so bad, crying so hard, and he begged me to see him. His mother had just died. He needed me, and"—I tore my eyes from his—"I thought I could save him." That was the reality of that night, the reason I'd ultimately left. "And, yes, I did love him, but I wasn't in love with him." I didn't go into the details of that night. Josh didn't need to know about all the lies and women and drugs and my stupidity.

The pupils in his eyes darkened, and then his focus was intently on my face, as though he were observing me. Time seemed to slow down, and we were both out of words. He took one step forward into my personal space.

"Red or blue?" he whispered.

"What?" I asked, confused and on the edge of breaking down right in front of him.

"Icing on your cake. Red or blue?" His voice quieted.

I swallowed. "Blue."

"Ice cream or cake?" he went on.

"Josh." My voice quivered. My emotional state was shot.

"Ice cream or cake," he pressed, his jaw tense, his focus firm.

"Cake."

"Do you love him?" he choked out.

"No!" I yelled, frustrated and angry. With him, with myself, with the whole damn world.

"Are you still in love with me?" His eyes glossed over.

"Yes." I didn't want to play any more games. He needed to know the truth.

With a curt nod and his eyes serious, he stepped back and dropped to one knee, pulling out a square velvet box from his pocket.

Hands up, body shaking, tears falling in full force, I said, "No. No. No." My head shook from left to right. "You don't get to fix this, Josh. I'm not letting you do this."

And that was one of the reasons I had decided never to tell him. I had known he'd try to do the right thing when I'd wronged him in more ways than I could count.

"No," I said. More tears. More sobs. Even more regrets.

He swallowed hard, reaching his hands out to touch me. "What if I told you I had this ring for a while now." Slow breaths escaped him, as though he were trying to keep it together. "What if I told you, I've been carrying it in my pocket this whole time because . . ." The heel of his palm rubbed at the center of his chest. "Simply because I wanted to keep a part of you with me even though we were done."

"I'd say, I'm the one who screwed up, and you should take it back."

His figure was a distorted image behind my tears. No, I didn't deserve him. When you loved someone, you wanted the best for them, and I wasn't it.

He stuffed the ring in his back pocket, stood and grabbed my hand. He intertwined our fingers and pulled me into him, resting his forehead against mine. I had waited months for this, months to feel his touch again, and I was too weak to pull away. A better woman would have pulled away.

My eyes fell shut as I breathed him in, and our breaths were intermingled in the small span of space between us.

One touch.

One breath.

One exhale.

It reminded me of the first day I'd met him at the department store.

"Sometimes, it's so hard to love you, Sam." He lightly tapped his head against mine, his voice filling with emotion. "But you know what's harder?" When he cupped the side of my face, my eyes opened to meet his. "Trying to stop."

Love, adoration, and hurt poured out of him. A mixture of

emotions could be read through his transparent eyes.

"So, I want it to end. This internal war to stop loving you. Sometimes, I think it's better to hate you, but when I try, it doesn't work. Because the person I make up in my mind, that person I hate, is not the one I fell in love with. And, when I tell myself I can do better—because you hurt me, and I deserve better than that—my heart knows . . . I can't." His voice shook with conviction.

"And the world knows I've tried to get over you, but it sends me back right here, with you in my arms. When I'm here, I forget . . . I forget all that hurt." He winced. "Yeah, I'm afraid to get hurt again, but I'm fucking chancing it with you because, if there is anyone in this world made for me, it's you, Sam. You're my person." His lips touched my forehead. "And I want to spend forever, day in and day out, with you. With the baby."

His words melted me, but the reality of my world could not be ignored. "She might not be yours," I whispered, feeling agony like I'd never felt in my life.

"You think I came here, not knowing that? I know that. And if . . ." He wrapped his hands tighter against mine. "If there's a chance that baby growing inside you *is* mine, I want that chance to love her, to bring the baby up right, by your side because that's how I always pictured us."

"But what if she's not?" I whispered, my true fears pushing through. "You going to live with that?"

He stepped back, his face thoughtful. With one light finger, he lifted my chin to meet his eyes. "Yes." His voice was resolute, his eyes firm. "Because, even if there is no part of me in that child of yours, she's still a part of you, and I want to love every part of you." He placed his hands on my stomach. "Even this part."

Where had this living angel fallen from?

"Josh . . ." I protested.

"Are you in love with me, Samantha Clarke?" he asked, his voice strong.

Through tear-filled eyes, I couldn't answer.

"It's a simple question."

"Of course I am. I never stopped loving you," I croaked out.

He cupped the side of my face. "Then, we'll find a way to get back to where we were. It'll take time, but we'll get there. Okay?" He rested his head against mine. "Do you want this?"

I nodded. "I do."

"Me, too."

Then, he closed the gap between us and kissed me. It was only a light brush of our lips, but it ignited the same fire in my veins, it increased my pulse, it made my whole body tingle. The effect that Josh had on me had not dimmed. If anything, it grew stronger.

chapter THIRTEEN

THE NEXT FEW WEEKS WENT by slowly.

When I wasn't at work and Josh wasn't in school, we were together. Going to the movies, eating, and baking. It was as if we were dating all over again, but we weren't quite there. Josh had been taking our relationship painfully slow. But, for once, I was taking his lead.

At times, I'd be down on myself, guilt-ridden. And, at other times, Josh would be angry with me, like it was hard to forget what I had done to him.

But we made a pact to talk about it when our feelings overfilled our emotional buckets. If we built a good foundation, we would last. The foundation that we had originally formed had obliterated because of the earthquake I had caused. And I made a secret oath to live my life redeeming myself.

We were both plopped on the couch, watching a game show I wasn't paying attention to, when my mind wandered, like it had been doing a lot recently.

When he placed his hand on my belly, my eyes met his.

"Do we have a name yet?" he asked, a dimple popping on his cheek.

I had missed that dimple.

"Not sure."

He bent down and began talking to my stomach, his new fascination lately, "Hey, pretty baby. What should we name you?"

I bit my bottom lip from quivering because, in another life and another time, one where I had made better decisions, this would be a happy moment.

He sat up and lightly tapped my head with his finger. "What are you thinking up there?"

I shook my head and blinked back tears. *Damn hormones.*

He gathered me in his arms, holding me snugly. "When you get all quiet, I know a storm is building up in that little blonde head of yours. So, just tell me what you're thinking. You promised."

"Don't you ever wonder what you'll do . . . if she's not yours?"

He blinked and stared at me for far too long without saying anything. "My sister hates you and still doesn't know we're back together. My friends think I'm just plain stupid. Everyone is telling me to forget you. Problem was . . . I tried. I had to make a decision. Walk away or accept every single part of you."

Just as he finished what he was saying, the door to his apartment flew open, and my whole body tensed. Casey stood a few feet away from me. The color drained from her face, and her eyes filled with fury.

"You're fucking kidding me, right?" she said. "Will slipped and told me you were back together with her."

I wished I could block out her irate voice, but I couldn't because I deserved it. I deserved to hear her wrath.

Josh's eyes dashed toward his sister. He stood and gripped her elbow, angling her away from me. "Casey, listen, we will talk about this later."

"No!" She propped her hands on her hips. "Are you dumb? She's pregnant. You haven't been together in months. Is it even yours? Is it?" She threw words at him like stones.

He didn't answer, but he pulled Casey into his room. I could still hear them though because his door wasn't shut all the way.

I released a heavy sigh. Maybe I needed to leave. But there was nothing that she could say that I didn't already know. I stood, and just when I thought she'd convince him to leave me, his words stopped me.

"She's it, Case."

A pleading cry broke from her lips. "She's not. Listen to me." Her voice heightened with deep family emotion. "You, big bro, can have any woman you want. Anyone! They'd drop to your feet. It's not only your good looks . . . it's your heart, Josh. It's a heart made of gold, and she doesn't deserve it."

My hand flew to my parted mouth, as I was unable to stay steady because it was the truth, all of it. I didn't deserve him. He deserved so much better than me . . . someone faithful and kind and selfless, just like he was.

"It's got to be her. Those months . . . those months that I was away from her, I thought of her the whole time. I love her, Casey. And I went on dates. Shit, a whole lot of them. But it didn't help. Going out with other girls only proved one thing . . . that I don't want to be with anybody else."

"Josh, you just need time."

"No, see, that's just it. It doesn't matter. There's no amount of time that will ever get me over her because I don't want to. Look at Dad. It's been years, Casey."

Josh's voice was so clear, so powerful, making a case to his own sister. "You told me . . . when grandfather forced my hand with the business, you told me, it's my life. Well, I'm telling you, it's my life, and if I walk away right now, if I just upped and left her . . . it would be because I was living how you wanted me to live and how my friends wanted me to live. Because how I want to live . . . it's with that woman out there . . . forever."

"Josh," she said, "you deserve so much better. Don't do this."

"You don't understand, Case. A few weeks ago, I was at a crossroads in my life." His voice shook with emotion. "Where I struggled with an internal battle. I was at that pizza joint, and I didn't even see her. I felt her, crazy as it sounds." He laughed without humor. "I turned, and there she was. I left Will sitting at the table and approached her. Shit. And the first thing I wanted to do was reach for her hand because I wanted confirmation that she was really there, like the first time I'd met her. Because, in the darkness, through a lineup, I could pick her hand from the softness of her skin and the lines on her palm."

His voice lowered where I strained to hear him. "Then, I saw her. Pregnant. And, for a brief second, just a second, I was so sure it was mine. Until she told me she wasn't sure."

"Josh," Casey started, as though she didn't want to hear any more.

But he only continued, "I started to walk home. I aimlessly walked around and around in the city. And, when I looked up, do you know where I ended up?" He let out a low laugh. "I ended up in front of her place."

I breathed through his next words, feeling unworthy.

"If you love me, Case, you'll let me decide how to live my life."

Silence ensued after that.

Who knew what was being said? The only people who knew the outcome of their conversation were the two people in the room.

When they exited the room, Casey didn't acknowledge my existence. She hugged Josh one last time and walked out the door without throwing a glance my way.

I blew out a breath and kept my eyes steady on the TV, pretending I hadn't just overheard their whole conversation.

"So . . . that was interesting, wasn't it?" he asked, his tone light.

"Yeah."

When I peered at him, he pulled me onto his lap and dropped his head into the crook of my neck, his arms wrapping around my belly.

"Don't worry about Casey."

I quirked an eyebrow at his nonchalance.

This man would fight the world for me. I only wished I deserved it.

The warmth of his lips touched my bare neck. "Life is about choices. And these choices have consequences. I figure there are two doors that I can choose from. If I walk away, you'll meet someone, and I'll meet someone. Then, we'll move on. We'll live separate lives. Thing is . . . I'd rather take this door that leads to you."

It was too much. With me being pregnant and his undying devotion, it was all too much to handle.

I grabbed his ears and pulled him into me, kissing him full force. "I love you. So much. I promise never to hurt you again. I promise." My eyes bore into his.

"Do you?" he asked, his fingers branding my sides.

I knew above anything that there was no one out there better for me than him. "Yes," I replied with certainty and conviction.

He lightly traced a path from my temple and down my cheek, resting on my bottom lip. His eyes took me in, memorizing my every feature. I breathed him in, his musky cologne and everything that was my Josh.

A small smile touched his face before he angled closer and kissed my nose. Then, my lips. Just a peck. But the soft kiss triggered tingles throughout my whole body, from down my neck and a direct line to my core.

Slow pecks turned into nibbles against the tender part of my bottom lip, and it transformed into his whole mouth on mine. His kisses sparked a fire in my belly. His lips devoured me, as though I were a gourmet meal—only this time, he was the cook.

When he pulled back, I read a look of longing and passion and need that mirrored mine.

The air around us seemed electrified, and my heart danced with excitement, knowing this was it.

The next second, he stood and pulled me up. When he bent down and his arms flew under my knees, I protested because I was packing an extra twenty pounds, but he only silenced me with his lips. He swept me up like I was weightless in his arms, and my whole body trembled with desire of what was to come.

He walked us back to his room and gently guided me onto my back on top of his bed.

"Josh." I wanted him so much, more than my next breath. I loved this man beyond my own comprehension.

My hands threaded through his hair as he hovered over me, careful not to smash my belly. I wasn't that overly plump yet, but my pooch was noticeably round.

"I've missed you so much." His voice was gruff and warm against my skin.

When his thumbs flicked over my nipples covered by my black lace bra, I arched my back, needing to get closer and wanting the itchy barrier between us off.

He knelt on the bed, and with one hand, he reached for the back of his shirt and lifted it over his head. I rested back on my elbows, taking in the sight of his beautiful body. My mouth watered at his well-defined six-pack and the glorious muscles and lines right above his hip bones. I wanted to run my tongue along his taut muscles.

"See something you like?" A sexy-ass dimple appeared on his face as he witnessed me gawking.

I bit my lip and nodded. Then, I reached for the waistband of his jeans. "Pregnant women are especially horny. I wanted to jump your bones weeks ago," I said, honesty leaking out of me.

He licked the seam of his lips and seductively peered down at me. Then, he gently guided himself above me, the veins in his forearms popping out. "Is that so?"

"Yes," I said, breathless.

He was teasing me, tempting me, and prolonging the inevitable.

He unbuttoned my jeans at a painfully slow pace and tugged them along with my panties down my legs. Then came my shirt and my bra.

When he slipped a finger in me, I gasped. Our eyes locked as he created this sensual friction with the magic of his skilled fingers.

With his mouth, he sucked on my breast, while watching me through hooded eyes.

The passion in me rose, clouding my brain. The increasing thrusts of his fingers awakened flames deep inside me. The beginning of a sensation at the bottom of my spine spread to my toes, and I knew I was so close to combustion, but it wasn't enough.

I pulled at his hand. "I want you inside me when I come."

Nice and slow was long gone. Fast and furious took its place. I pulled at the button of his jeans at the same time he unbuttoned the clasp of my bra.

Our hands, our lips moved with purpose and a hungry desire. He pulled me to the edge of the bed and pressed his tip against my wetness. With one thrust, he entered me with a raw act of possession.

I was his, and he was mine.

The heat of his palms gripped the swell of my hips, and all I could hear was the slapping of skin on skin. All I could smell was the aroma of our heat. All I could feel was Josh. All of him.

When his movements increased in urgency, that familiar sensation initiated at the base of my spine.

"Harder," I breathed, needing to feel more of him.

He pushed into me with a ravenous frenzy until the convulsions took over, and my body began to vibrate with liquid passion. With one last thrust, both of us came together in utter ecstasy, pure nirvana.

The heat in my body spread to my heart. Our connection carried an intensity so strong, it took a while for us to come down from the ultimate high.

When our breathing evened out and our pulse returned to a normal rate, he pulled me into him, spooning me against him, his hands gently placed on our baby.

Ours.

Because that was what he'd decided. I'd have to learn to accept his decision, and eventually, I could forgive myself.

But the thought of his sacrifice and loving me brought such emotion to the surface that tears fell from my eyes. When I was with him, everything in the world seemed right again. I'd been walking in a world thrown off its axis, but with Josh, I was centered, steady.

When I sniffled against my own will, Josh peered over at me. "What's wrong?" The warmth in his smile echoed in his tone. "That bad, huh? Well, I'm in need of some practice. Next time will be better."

I shook my head, too emotional to give him an answer. Lately, I'd been a hormonal mess.

He brushed an escaping strand of hair from my face. It tingled where he touched.

When I continued to cry, his smile slowly faltered, his eyes turning serious. "You're not going to want for anything. You and the baby." His voice cracked with emotion. "Whatever he can give you, I'll give you more. Because the difference is, I'm here. I'm going to be here, be present. I'm going to hold you when you cry, and I'm going to experience every happy moment with the both of you."

I lifted my head and kissed him deeply. "I'm not crying about that. I'm crying because I have a second chance. Because I'm so happy."

He brushed his nose against mine. "Me, too, Princess. Me, too."

He pulled me against him and held me in silence.

Though an hour had passed, I knew he was still awake, probably wondering, like me, about everything we'd been through but glad that we'd still made it here—in each other's arms.

Warmth surrounded us, the type that radiated from the inside out. My breathing slowed against Josh's chest as he continually brushed my hair with his fingers.

And, as I feigned sleep, he whispered, "Samantha Clarke." I felt the compressions of his chest against my cheek cease, and he stopped breathing completely. "I love you." His voice was soft, yet it exuded such strength, and I knew he meant those words with his whole being.

As his breathing evened out until he was soundly sleep, a single tear escaped my eye because I knew this was real.

Love wasn't fleeting. It didn't excite you one minute and die out the next. That was lust. This was everlasting. A love that stood by you for a thousand years.

Love lifted you up, and at times, love was hard. It was a sacrifice and sacrificed for you, but to be loved and to love was utter bliss.

Josh was love. Every part of him confirmed that love existed. His selflessness. His ability to forgive. His ability to see the truth in all people and to love with his whole heart.

I didn't deserve him, and as he'd said that he would never find anyone better than me . . . the truth was, there was no man better than him. No one.

I had to believe there was a God.

Because everything happened for a reason.

chapter FOURTEEN

Three Years Later

IN MY LIVING ROOM AND on my knees, I stuffed Gracie's belongings into her baby bag. A sippy cup, Pull-Ups, and wipes were all I needed.

Josh strolled in with his suit jacket on and his tie in his hand. "Where's Gracie?"

I tipped my head to our small family room where our three-year-old was engrossed in a session of *Mickey Mouse Clubhouse*.

"Crack TV." I grinned and zipped up the bag.

Our two-bedroom apartment was packed like a sardine with all of Gracie's toys. Our living room functioned as her toy room with her kitchen set and all her plates and food shoved against the side of the couch.

When I stood, my breath caught.

Josh took me in, as though he were seeing me for the first time, photographing me with his eyes. He bit his fist and strolled toward me. "Hot damn, woman."

Butterflies flittered and fluttered in my stomach. They always did when he gave me *the* look.

My hands flattened the front of my black skirt suit. It had been years since I'd been in a suit. My body felt confined. Thank goodness I'd only be wearing it for the interview.

It had taken me two years to finish school at Le Cordon Bleu. After a heap of loans, lack of sleep, and the support of my husband,

I had done it. He had pushed me to pursue my dreams and hadn't stopped hounding me until I did. Now, it was just a matter of getting myself back into the kitchen and back to work.

"I'm nervous." Honesty leaked out of my mouth, and my hands fidgeted at the edge of my skirt.

He smiled—one dimple, not two, the smile that told me I was being ridiculous.

"You? Nervous?" Josh's hands snaked around my waist and pulled me into him. He released a low, hoarse whistle. "I'm the one who's nervous. Look at you. I won't be there to keep the men away."

A blush touched my cheeks. After three years of marriage, Josh still made me feel beautiful and wanted. "Please . . . I only have eyes for you."

We had married in his small chapel back home, the one his parents had gotten married in. It had been an intimate affair with his father, Casey, and Chloe in attendance. It was important to Josh that we were married before the baby was born, and it was important to me that he was happy.

With his fingertips, he lifted my chin and pecked me on the lips. When he pulled me closer against him, his kiss lingered, and I breathed my husband in, his signature musky cologne mixed with the scent of his shampoo. I wrapped both arms around his neck, and his kiss deepened when he flicked his tongue against the seam of my lips.

"I have a solution that could relax you," he said, his tone sexy and seductive.

I sighed into him. I was ovulating, but I didn't have the time today.

As soon as Gracie had turned one, we'd started trying for another baby but had no luck. Sometimes, it seemed as though the world was against us. Every month, it was the same disappointment—no baby.

But Josh's baby-making motto pushed to the surface. *"We'll keep trying until we get it right. Practice makes perfect."*

I wrapped my arms tighter around him. "I so want round two, but we can't. I'm going to be late."

He smirked and dropped his lips to my neck instead. "You're probably right." He nipped at the tender spot of my neck and let out a low laugh.

"After the interview, I promise," I said.

It had been years since I'd stepped into a restaurant as a chef. I hadn't spent thousands on school to bake pastries for our neighbors and family friends. I wanted to get back in the game. Gracie was going into preschool, and I was ready to get back to work. Also, we needed the money.

Working for a nonprofit organization did not pay well enough to support a family of three. Though he never admitted it, I could tell Josh was stressed about finances. It was in the stiffness of his shoulders as he'd sit at his desk, paying the monthly bills, and his soft sighs when he'd open our mail.

And I wanted to financially contribute to our family. He had been supporting me in more ways than I could count since I'd delivered, and now, it was my turn to give back.

He bent me backward, kissed me one last time, and then set me back on my feet. "You're going to do great." His eyes twinkled with a confidence I wish I had. "Be yourself, and I swear, you'll get the job. I'm sorry I can't take Gracie."

I waved one hand. "Stop. You'll be in court today, and those parents need you. Chloe said she'd meet me at the restaurant and take Gracie for an hour. It's not like these types of things last longer than that. If I get a second interview, then they'll have me in the kitchen. I'll know in advance, and you can take her then."

He nodded, but I could still see the reluctance in his eyes. "All right, let's go. You don't want to be late." He winked. "I'll put her in the car."

He turned toward our munchkin, reached down, and threw her in the air like a little human football. Her giggles were contagious and had both of us laughing. Her blondish curly hair was in disarray and bounced as she hit the air. Some would call it messy, but I couldn't worry about it anymore. I had tried everything to tame her unruly hair, and she hated her curls being tied back, so we let it run wild. Josh, on the other hand, said her hair had character, just like her—wild and free.

I bit my cheek. *Wild and free.*

Little things would spark memories of her father. Not memories of longing, but the realization that the wild and free in our little Gracie that could not be tamed had come from him.

I didn't think of Hawke often, but when I did, my stomach would clench with anxiety.

Josh zipped up her jacket and put on her Hello Kitty shoes. "We're ready to go, Mom."

She peeked out from under her oversize Mickey hat and smiled, showing two dimples that were so like Josh's but weren't really his.

"Okay, let's do this." I slipped the baby bag and my purse over the same shoulder.

"First things first. Family hug to make Mama feel better." Josh wrapped his arms around me, and we squeezed.

"Mama hug, *pweese*." Gracie snuggled in between us. We were making a human sandwich where we were the bread and she was the meat.

I let her laughter wash over me and calm my nerves, and it worked like it always did. Josh and Gracie had the ability to do that, just by being them.

As I drove downtown, nursery rhymes played in the background. Gracie and I belted out the words to "The Wheels on the Bus," as though I were Adele and she was my backup. God, I loved my simple suburban life.

When I dropped the car at the valet and grabbed Gracie, I was on a high that could not be broken. I walked into the restaurant, confident that I was going to slay the interview.

I reached for my phone in my pocket. I didn't have to dial Chloe's number because she stood from a table in front of me, calm, collected, and on time. Her striped suit hugged her slim runner figure. With a grin, she rushed toward me and reached for Gracie without even a hello my way.

"Auntie Coo." Gracie's eyes lit up at her godmother.

Chloe showered her face with kisses, not caring that she was getting lipstick all over my baby's face.

"Hello to you, too, Chloe," I sassed.

Her eyes appraised me. "Wow. You look great, Sam. I don't remember the last time I saw you in a suit."

"I don't remember the last time I saw *me* in a suit."

We both laughed.

Chloe stared at Gracie with a look of adoration. "I hope it's okay"—Chloe rubbed her nose against Gracie's, which made her giggle—"I figured I'd eat lunch here and spend fairy godmother and Gracie time together. If she starts to get antsy, I'll leave, and you can just call me."

I nodded. "Sounds good." I doubted my interview would last longer than thirty minutes anyway.

The restaurant was packed with its normal patrons. It wasn't a super fancy place where you couldn't bring children, but it definitely held a four-star ambiance, and I doubted children were here on the weekends.

Black velvet couches lined the edges of the room while round tables sat in the center, all decked in white linen and full place settings. The decor exuded modern sophistication, something the regular chain restaurants in our suburbs did not have.

I peered down at my watch. I had five minutes. "All right, I'm going to head up now. Wish me luck."

Chloe winked and readjusted Gracie on her hip. "No luck

needed. You're going to kill it."

I kissed Gracie on the head and flattened out my skirt. With my portfolio in hand, I walked to the bar. Butterflies took flight in my stomach, making me feel unsteady, but it was now or never.

I approached the bartender as instructed in the email and said, "Hi, I'm Samantha Stanton. I'm here for an interview with Juan."

The bartender had shoulder-length jet-black hair that shone under the light. "Yes, follow me," she said, her tone friendly.

I trailed behind her, feeling the ridge of my portfolio against the inside of my palm. I pictured Josh telling me his favorite phrase.

"Exhale, Sam."

And so I did.

This is it.

FORTY-FIVE MINUTES LATER, JUAN, THE head pastry chef, shook my hand. "See you next week in the kitchen."

I grinned, unable to contain my excitement. "It was a pleasure." I firmly shook his hand. "Thank you so much. I'll see you next week."

There was a skip in my step, and I had to control the urge not to sprint to Chloe's table.

I clasped my hands together and jumped. "Chloe . . ." I peered behind me to see if Juan had made his way back to the kitchen. When he did, I squeed at her, "I landed a second interview. They want to see me next week!"

Her eyes brightened, and her smile widened, almost as big as mine. "Oh, hell yeah."

We high-fived.

I pointed to Gracie who had Chloe's phone in her hand and earbuds on her ears.

"Tupac," Chloe blurted with such a straight face that I narrowed my eyes at her.

She reeled back and raised an incredulous eyebrow. "Hello? What kind of godmother do you think I am?"

I chuckled. "No comment."

Then, my eyes zoned in on Mickey Mouse playing on the screen.

"We ate already but did you want to order something?" she asked.

My insides wanted to explode, and all I wanted to do was call Josh, but he was already in court. "Sure, let me text the hubs first."

I texted Josh but didn't get a response. When he did see my text, there was no doubt I would get a phone call.

When my adrenaline tapered off, I sat down, placed my cell on the table, and opened the menu, my stomach already grumbling at the anticipation of getting fed. I hadn't eaten breakfast like I normally did, being so nervous, but now that the butterflies had subsided, my appetite was back in full swing, and I picked at Chloe's leftover fries.

Chloe filled me in about the most recent guy she was dating. I knew she was looking for the right one, but all the wrong ones had kept showing up at her door. At times, I'd see the longing in her eyes when she looked at Gracie or when I was with Josh. She had said she wasn't searching for the type of life Josh and I had, but sometimes, I read something deeper behind her eyes.

After ordering, I filled Chloe in on every question Juan had thrown my way. When Gracie said she had to go potty, I rushed her to the restroom. She had a Pull-Up on, but I didn't want to risk any accidents, especially at my future place of employment.

She finished, and as a reward, I kissed her cheek and dug into my pocket for a lollipop. We'd been rewarding her with kisses and candy. Or maybe the kisses were our reward for having such a sweet child.

I held her hand as we walked out of the bathroom, and in Gracie-esque fashion, she skipped and smiled up at me. I was so enamored by her that I didn't notice the crowd gathering at the front.

I realized we were at the peak of rush hour, and Gracie's nap was coming, an indication that I needed to leave soon.

When I approached the table, Chloe's eyes widened with alarm. When I saw the flashes of light coming from outside, a memory triggered in my brain, but I couldn't quite piece it together.

Then, my skin prickled with awareness, my throat fell dry, and my heartbeat picked up in my chest. The mood shifted in the air, and the moment slowed.

Time stood still.

A spike of terror hit me when I saw a familiar tall, broad male, whose upper body reminded me of a football player, strolling in.

Tilton.

Without thinking, I swooped Gracie up, bringing her toward my chest and hiding her face.

My eyes darted around the room for anywhere to go, for anywhere to hide, for anywhere to disappear. My breathing picked up in pace, and it was like I was having hot flashes. Not knowing what to do next, I rocked back in place, as though I were putting Gracie to sleep even though she was fully awake.

Tilton's eyes widened with surprise when his eyes made it toward my direction. I could tell by the way his body was blocking my view that he didn't want me to be seen either, but then the crowd parted like the Red Sea, and a familiar pair of green eyes locked on mine.

After the initial shock, Hawke smiled, and his whole face brightened.

Mine fell.

My fingers dug into Gracie's back, the slight movement causing his eyes to flicker to her. I was frozen. The only body parts moving were my arms gripping Gracie against me.

He swaggered toward me at his signature cool pace.

At one time, I had adored him. At one time, Hawke's presence had had my heart racing and my mouth watering. At one time, the need to touch him had been overwhelming, and being with him had breathed life into me.

But not now.

Now, fear shook my body with each step he took toward me, like a dangerous lion approaching its prey.

The reaction to run was so strong that I had to force my feet to stay and force my face to keep steady.

"Sunshine . . ." One word that used to send shivers down my spine, now filled the back of my throat with bile.

He glanced again at Gracie, my baby, *our* baby. Gracie's head rested on my shoulder, away from the chaos in front of me.

I couldn't move. I couldn't form words. I couldn't respond to the man who was about to change my life.

My words were lodged in the back of my throat, coated with a thickness I couldn't swallow down.

Chloe bumped me and stood between us. "Hawke? Is that you? I didn't recognize you. You look . . . different."

The way she said *different* wasn't a good thing.

Because it wasn't.

He'd lost a lot of weight, and the bags were heavy under his eyes.

"Gracie, come over here, sweetness." Chloe extracted Gracie from my arms. Thankfully, she went without a peep. "Thanks, Sam, for taking her to the restroom, so I could eat. I can tell she's tired. It's her nap time, so I'll just be over here."

The air released in one large swish from my lungs. I wondered if he'd heard it.

He furrowed his eyebrows, darting his gaze between the three of us, but I used Chloe's reprieve to divert his attention.

"Hey . . ." I waved at him.

He turned my way and smirked. And, from his disregard of our child, I knew he hadn't gotten a good look at her.

"After all these years, is that all I get?" He closed the gap between us.

I gave him a noncommittal half-hug, but he held me tighter, breathing me in and holding me close.

I let out a silent sigh once Chloe and Gracie were back at their table.

In his arms, I didn't feel butterflies, nor did I feel disappointment or anger. All I felt was an emptiness, as though I were hugging a stranger.

"You look great."

I sensed longing in his tone, like he'd meant to say, *I missed you.*

But I didn't miss him.

His whole body relaxed into me, like he was using me for a crutch, but I wasn't that girl anymore. I had grown up.

I slowly extracted myself from his hold and stepped back, needing space, needing air, needing to be away from him. His face had aged over the years that I hadn't seen him. Lines crinkled his forehead, and wrinkles outlined his eyes. And, in the deepest part of me, though I couldn't be entirely sure, I had a gut feeling he was still using.

"So . . . you're here for a concert?" I asked carefully.

Hopefully, he'd be gone in a few days, and we'd never cross paths again.

His eyes drank me in, the same way he did years ago when we were the same two young people who had met at a club.

But things were different now. My life was different now. I was different now.

I shifted from my unease.

"Yeah. In Chicago for a couple of days." He tipped his head and motioned with one hand toward my ensemble. "Where's your apron?"

"I just interviewed for a job here."

"New job?"

I nodded. He hadn't known that I had quit my old one because of Gracie.

"Yeah. Better pay." I crossed both fingers in the air. "Upscale restaurant. I hope I get the job."

He sucked on his bottom lip, and his eyes scoured my body. "You'll get it." His intense stare was predatory and had me drawing back and wanting to hide in a corner. "You look great," he repeated.

"Thanks."

A whole lot of awkward filled the air, which forced my gaze to the ground.

"I called you a bunch of times." His voice quieted to a hush, as though he didn't want anyone to know but only wanted for me to hear.

Still not meeting his gaze, I said, "Yeah, I know. It was for the best."

"I didn't like how we left things."

No apologies came from his mouth. But it was okay because that was my past.

"It's fine. That was years ago."

"Still."

He reached for my hand, his eyes dropping to my ring. "You still with Josh?"

I retracted my hand from his because he had no right to touch me anymore. "How do you know that I'm Josh's? How do you know it wasn't someone else?"

He shrugged. "Lucky guess? Or maybe I've been keeping tabs on the love of my life."

Too much. Too fast. And all lies.

"Hawke, don't," I said, my tone meaning business.

"What do you want me to say? That I don't think of you? Or of us?" His eyes softened, almost making his words believable but not quite.

I wasn't having this conversation. Ever. I didn't reciprocate his feelings.

He'd hurt me, but what came out of my mouth next was not meant to hurt him. It was the absolute truth.

"I'm happy with Josh. Actually, I've never been happier."

His demeanor changed, his smile dimming, like I'd doused him with cold water. If he'd thought I would fall over one of his lines, he was dead wrong. I had fallen for him when I was twenty-three naive and not knowing about the world. I wasn't twenty-three anymore. To be young and in love was dumb.

He nodded toward my ring. "I could've gotten you a bigger one."

He was so full of shit. I gritted my teeth and realized he hadn't changed. He still thought money could buy him everything, but I couldn't be bought.

I lifted my chin and pushed my shoulders back. "It's okay. He's much bigger and more than enough for me to handle." I was no longer speaking about the ring.

When I clenched my jaw, he laughed.

My words were meant to hurt him, but I should have known from experience that nothing hurt him.

"It's good to see you haven't changed, and you're still the jokester I knew." His eyes squinted and lit with humor.

"It's sad to see you haven't," I said, crossing my arms over my chest.

His eyebrows gathered in, almost looking regretful. Our banter stopped, and silence ensued. He stood, unsmiling, as his eyes took in my face.

I was about to say my good-byes, end this chapter for good, when I heard, "Mama . . ."

The voice of a sweet angel broke our intense connection.

I blinked and turned toward my daughter. My masked composure turned to full-blown panic. Chloe, bewildered and shaking, chased Gracie, who was rushing toward me.

Everything happened in slow motion, as though I were watching it on a big screen.

My breath hitched in my throat. I swooped her up and held her to my chest. Hawke's facial features changed like a deck of cards. Happiness, curiosity, and then, for the first time ever, shock filled his face when Gracie turned toward him and stuck her sucker in her mouth.

His eyes went wide as he took her in. He focused on her, unbreathing and unblinking and unmoving. His mouth fell open, and a gasp escaped, loud enough for me to hear.

Then, his eyes turned to me. Wonder and questions that I didn't want to answer spanned his face.

"Gracie, come to Mama," Chloe said, her voice quivering.

There was no point. It was too late.

My insides heightened with hysteria, and my limbs were visibly trembling as I said, "Hawke, have fun at your concert."

I maintained composure as I walked swiftly out the door, but I it was all for nothing because he knew.

It was undeniable.

It was in the dirty blonde in her hair.

It was the grassy green in her eyes.

They held all the same features.

He knew Gracie was his daughter.

And I was scared shitless.

chapter FIFTEEN

I PACED OUR LIVING ROOM and pressed my hand against my stomach.

After I'd put Gracie in her big-girl bed for her nap, I'd cried. I hadn't cried in such a long time. There had been no reason to. There was no drama in my life. Josh and Gracie filled my life with a joy that could not be measured or described in words.

Who knew why I was crying? Angry tears? If I had to guess, I was crying tears of fear. Fear of the unknown. Fear of our future, Gracie's future.

I knew I'd been in the wrong for keeping Hawke from Gracie all these years, but in my heart, I wanted to protect her. I wasn't ready for her to live her life with her biological father's lifestyle.

What would her life have consisted of if I had told Hawke? What would that have exposed her to?

And, by the time that I had delivered and known that Gracie was his, it was too late. Josh had been a father to her months before her birth. Josh had loved her when he felt her first kick in my stomach. He'd loved her when he saw her on the ultrasound machine. He'd loved her when she came out of my womb, and he'd cut the cord, staring into green eyes that were neither of ours or any of our family members.

I had been fine with not telling Hawke because I was never, ever supposed to see him again. I never wondered about him. I never cared about what he was doing. The only thing I cared about was that he would not interfere with our lives.

Fear clouded my mind as I paced the room, trying to think of a game plan. Hawke Calvin had never been denied what he wanted. Whatever he wanted, he took. But over my dead body would he take Gracie from me or from Josh.

Thoughts filtered through my mind because I knew the resources he had access to. He was probably calling the best lawyers out there, weighing his options.

If anything, this would be good promo for him.

Once this secret leaked, it would turn my quiet world upside down. Again.

When the door flew open, I cupped my mouth, trying to contain my tears, but Josh saw. The smile fell from his face, and he dropped the bouquet of flowers in his hand, rushing to my side.

Automatically, I was in his arms.

He didn't deserve this.

With a light hand, he cupped my cheek and searched my face. "I thought you got a second interview."

The absurdity of his statement had me burying my face into his shirt further. Like I would be this upset over something so miniscule.

He rested his chin on my head, and I fisted the back of his shirt, pulling him closer.

"What happened?"

"I saw *him*." My voice quivered into a broken mess, and from those few words, he knew.

My cheek rested on his chest as he stopped breathing. No air was entering or leaving his lungs. His whole body was statue still.

He pulled back, studied my face, and then his mouth turned downward. He blew out a shallow breath and stepped away from me. The abrupt movement almost had me falling to the floor.

"Where?"

"The restaurant. He was just there after my interview. For lunch." I swiped at my cheeks to dry them, but it was no use.

His eyes flew behind himself to her bedroom. This wasn't about me seeing my ex-boyfriend. The stakes were higher now. We both had everything to lose.

With one hand, he gripped the tips of his hair, making it stand on end. "He knows, doesn't he?"

I nodded as more tears escaped me.

The vein in Josh's temple pulsed, his normally calm demeanor diminishing. "What does he want?"

My elbows pressed against my sides as I tried to keep myself together, keep myself upright, but it was too much. I walked and fell against the couch. "I don't know. I didn't even give him a chance to say anything. I just left."

I dropped my head into my hands, feeling the wetness touch every part of my face.

The couch dipped, and warmth surrounded me again. He untangled my hands and lifted my chin with his fingertips.

"I'm sorry," I said, sobbing.

Two words that I meant so much, but over time, they had lessened in value. I was sorry for bringing this drama into our lives. I was sorry for hurting him. Most of all, I was sorry that Gracie wasn't his.

"I'm sorry for all of it."

He knew I was talking about more than what had happened today.

"Stop." Josh leaned into me, and his hands gently squeezed my knees. "Quit saying you're sorry. I don't know why you can't forgive yourself when I forgave you a long time ago. This has got to stop."

"If I didn't . . ."

"Then, Gracie wouldn't be here."

He was right.

My one night of guilt sex with Hawke was not supposed to happen. I couldn't go so far as to say that I wished it had never happened because the outcome of that night was Gracie, and she had given me happiness and fulfillment like I'd never felt before.

"But, you know, this is still your fault." His eyes danced with a light humor that made my heart ache.

His words caught me off guard.

But he smiled for my benefit. "I told you, you look good in that suit."

My face crumbled, and he pulled me onto his lap.

"He hit on you, didn't he? Never mind, I already know." His lips brushed against my temple. "The one guy . . . the only guy in the whole world who could take everything that's ever mattered to me . . ." He let out a long breath, tightening his hold on me. "But I'll be damned if I let that happen." With his voice firm, he exuded calm and focus. He pulled back and brushed his nose against my nose. "You're mine. Gracie's mine. I don't care about anything else. Love has no limitations. Not for me, it doesn't. And my love for you and Gracie is limitless. I'm not going to let anything happen to either of you."

Josh reached for his phone in his back pocket and I moved off his lap. He stood, pressed the phone to his ear and waited a moment.

And the person he called shocked me.

"Dad, we need to talk."

I blinked and stiffened, my posture rigid. Hearing Josh tell my father-in-law about my run-in with Hawke was putting a bad taste in my mouth.

Casey and I had passed that hump of her animosity toward me, but it had taken years to heal. Now, this would only bring up old wounds.

"Dad, I want to know what our options are. I might need your help."

I bit my tongue.

Josh never asked for help. His grandfather had disowned him, and though my father-in-law was not in cahoots with dear old grandpa, Josh had never asked his father for anything.

Josh was supporting us on his own, something he prided himself in. "I think we'll need a lawyer because this is a case that I'm too emotionally invested in to handle myself."

Where Hawke had money and fame, so did Josh but through his last name. By contacting his dad, I knew there was no stopping Josh from obtaining the top lawyer in the country to keep Gracie safe from Hawke's claws.

Courtroom intensity showed in Josh's eyes, letting me know he was going to fight until he won.

I only hoped it worked.

THAT NIGHT, I TOSSED AND turned and checked on Gracie multiple times. It wasn't like Hawke could sneak in and steal her from us, but the irrational side of me thought it was possible, and he would do just that—break in and take her while we were sleeping—because he always did what he wanted to.

I hugged Josh tightly the next morning when he left for work. After I dropped Gracie off at Aunt Casey's house to play with my newborn niece, I ran errands.

While I was emptying the contents of my grocery cart into the back of our Jeep Cherokee, a tall male in jeans and a button-down came up to my car.

"Excuse me," he said, getting my attention.

I smiled at him and placed the last bag of food in my Jeep. Carts were scarce in the middle of the day, so I gently pushed the cart in his direction. "All done," I said, smiling.

He pushed the cart away from himself. "Are you Samantha Stanton?"

I blinked, and my face features fell. "Yes."

"Miss Stanton I'm Chris, an associate from the Law Offices of John Bartlett, representing Hawke Calvin." A black file folder was in his hands. He looked no more than twenty-five with his slicked-back dark hair and casual business attire.

I shouldn't have been surprised, but I hadn't expected his lawyer to approach me in the middle of the grocery parking lot. And so soon.

An immediate wave of anger and protectiveness rushed over me. "Tell him to fuck off!"

I was surprised at my candor, but I couldn't help it. When my hand reached for the door handle, his words stopped me.

"Hawke Calvin and his lawyer, John Bartlett, would like to talk to you before legal proceedings begin."

I forced myself to face the messenger, and an internal debate stirred inside me. In one way, I should let our lawyer handle it, but a part of me wanted to face Hawke head-on.

The latter won, and I followed the lawyer's car to a high-rise on Michigan Avenue. In any other situation, I would have admired the grand architectural design of the place, but the prime location of the building only reminded me of the resources that Hawke had.

As the elevator climbed to the top floor, the lawyer tried to make small talk. My mind was reeling, and I wanted to call Josh, but I knew he'd leave court the moment I told him. A big part of me also wanted to settle this myself, save him from the pain.

After I stepped into a boardroom with floor-to-ceiling windows that gave a view of the whole city, the young lawyer exited and closed the door behind me. My jaw tightened when I spotted Hawke seated at the head of the table in torn jeans and a white cutoff T-shirt. A taller man with a crisp black suit sat beside him. He sported a full head of white hair, and his eyes were trained on me, already reading me from the moment I had entered the room. They both stood.

Hawke started to approach me, but I took a step back.

"It's great seeing you, Sunshine."

The way he uttered my nickname sent invisible spiders skittering over my skin.

"Why am I here?" I asked, eyes tight and voice hard.

Hawke sat back down, his eyes trained on me and his hands steepled by his lips. I sat across from him.

His high-paid lawyer's eyes were cautious. "Mrs. Stanton, I'm John Bartlett—"

When Hawke held up his hand, John stopped talking mid sentence.

I sat on the opposite end of the long mahogany table. The table was like a barrier between us, like a net in a volleyball game, dividing the opposing teams.

A deafening silence filled the room.

Hawke smiled and flicked something off the table, his eyes dropping from mine. "Pretty daughter you have there. Funny enough, I didn't think Shoe Boy had green eyes."

He'd met Josh once, so how the hell would he know?

My blood boiled, bubbling hot, and I inhaled deeply. "Actually, he does," I lied, smiling while I did it. "They're bluish-green," I said with the straightest face, unblinking, as if my life depended on that one sentence. And it did. Gracie was my life.

"I don't believe you." A malevolent smile surfaced. "Her age lines up with the last time we were together." He shrugged nonchalantly, as though it weren't a big deal to be playing with my life. "I guess we have to take a paternity test."

I lifted both brows, pretending I wasn't affected even though my pulse increased in tempo.

We had the longest staring contest known to man as my heartbeat thrashed loudly in my ears, causing a discomfort in my chest.

Then, it hit me.

He wasn't bluffing.

He was about to blow up our lives, and he'd be the one to walk away, unscathed.

I pointed a finger in his face. "Screw. You." I stood, and the chair flew back, tipping over.

I was normally calm but not now, not when he wanted to play God with my life. I refused to let him have power over my life anymore, and I'd be damned if he had power over my family.

"She's not yours. You hear me!" I stomped toward him, a foot away, my finger jabbing in his direction. "She's ours. Josh has raised her since she was an infant. Where were you? What were you doing?" My tone heightened in hysteria, and my arms flared at my sides. "Out screwing every girl with legs and getting so high that you forgot what you'd even done the night before? No! Do you hear me? No!"

His crooked smile had my blood pressure skyrocketing. "Sit down, Sunshine."

"Stop calling me that!"

"Sit down, Mrs. Stanton," Hawke's lawyer repeated.

"No!" I was so filled with rage, I couldn't see straight.

The pounding in my ears was deafening. The tremors in my body were overwhelming. It felt like everything was closing in on me, like walls narrowing together in a small room, making it difficult to get in my next breath.

"I'm going to talk to a lawyer and drag your ass through the media."

Hawke laughed without humor, which only infuriated me more. "You think I care about my pristine self-image? You know me, Sunshine. You've gotta come back with a better threat than that."

Tears burst from my eyes, and both hands flew to my lips. Damn it. I hated this. I hated the money he had access to. I hated him.

I didn't want to cry in front of him, but the emotions were overtaking me. He was going to hurt Josh all over again when he'd been hurt enough.

"I don't care," I wept. "I'll do everything in my power to keep you from her."

He stilled, unsure of what to do at the abrupt change in mood.

"I've never seen you this angry before. Even more now than that last night we were together," he said.

"I've never had anything to fight for before." I hugged my middle, barely standing straight. "What do you want? And don't say her because you can't have her."

"I want to know the truth." He leveled me with a stare. "Is she mine?"

Unable to hold myself up any longer, I fell to an empty chair. "Yes." The word rushed out and was barely above a whisper.

Gracie's beauty was a blessing and a curse. She looked exactly like her father with her high cheekbones and her emerald-green eyes with long lashes. She was her father's child through and through, and a judge would be able to determine that with one look at her. There was no need to take a paternity test.

But it didn't matter. She was Josh's. In her laughter and in her heart. In the way she was compassionate to everyone around her. That was all Josh. Josh and I had nurtured her to be who she was today. Hawke had had no part in that.

Silence overtook the room for a moment.

Then, I lifted my head and faced him dead-on, swallowing my leftover tears. "There. You have the truth. Are we done here?"

His green eyes bore into mine, all humor gone. The only emotions left in his eyes were pain and regret. "I had no idea. I knew you were with him, but"—he shook his head—"I had no idea."

That was exactly why I was not on social media. I had known he would search for me. I hadn't wanted to be found. What he didn't understand was that he was my past, Josh was my present, and Gracie was our future.

"Why didn't you tell me?"

I jutted out my chin in defiance. "Because it wasn't your right to know."

"Bullshit!" He gripped the chair hard, the veins in his forearms bulging. "She's my kid, Sunshine, and you tell me that I didn't have the right to know?" His look turned incredulous.

Gloves on. Bring it!

"What? Do you think the lifestyle you live is conducive to raising a child? How would knowing have changed anything? Would you have left the band? Given up your life and settled down to raise our child in suburbia?"

He opened his mouth to speak, but I pointed a finger in his direction. "Don't even say it. Don't even lie to me right now and tell me that you would have because we all know that's the real bullshit here. You wouldn't have. You don't care about anything or anyone but yourself. Are you going to tell me that you're clean now? You've been clean? Lie to my face all over again." I leveled my stare, my eyes hard and cold. "At the end of the day, it's all about you. What makes you feel good. What everyone can do for you." I didn't flinch as words, like daggers, shot directly at him. When I was done, I was breathless but weirdly satisfied at getting everything off my chest.

And, as I stared at the rock star, who had once and for a brief moment been *my* rock star, the only thing I felt was utter disgust.

There was no changing the circumstances. We could go around all day, but nothing was going to change. If Hawke wanted to fight for her, there was nothing I could do to change his mind. All I could do was prepare myself.

I picked up my purse, stood, and turned to his lawyer. "I'll have my lawyer call you."

I turned to Hawke, whose jaw was locked, his eyes unreadable.

I had to say one last thing. "Raising a child takes selflessness, which is something Josh has and you don't. As long as I'm living on this earth, your life will not taint our Gracie's. I promise you that." Then, I stormed out of there with my head high.

By the look in his eyes, I had just started a war. But I would fight to the death for my family.

I MADE IT ALL THE way through the revolving doors and outside. Taking in the tall glass skyscraper, I released a heavy sigh. The sun was out, and the birds were chirping, but nothing could erase the tightness in my chest.

Hawke would win this war because that was his right as a parent. I wouldn't fight him for that. She was half his after all. But even the idea of leaving her for a weekend with him killed me. The constant worry would always be there.

And what about Josh and the Stanton name?

By the time the press was done with this story, all of us would be dragged through the dirt and back. The only person who stood a chance at making it out of this situation was Hawke. The more tabloids they sold, the more money he'd make. The saying, *There's no such thing as bad publicity*, would only work toward his favor.

I closed my eyes and exhaled, one breath at a time. When I opened my eyes, clarity and desperation hit me. Once I left the vicinity, I wouldn't have another chance to talk to him before the legal circus began, so I stormed back into the building and into the conference room.

Hawke was shaking his lawyer's hand, and then his eyes went wide at my reappearance.

This time, it was my turn to be heard. "I want to speak to Hawke. Alone."

The lawyer's gaze ping-ponged between us. "I don't think that's advisable. It would be better—"

Hawke raised a hand, stopping his lawyer mid sentence. "Go." He was always the one to give orders, and everyone followed like a puppy.

The lawyer shook his head, but he left nonetheless.

The door shut, and Hawke slowly approached me as I stayed in my spot, formulating my next words. I needed to make them count.

He ran one hand through his hair. "I never wanted it to come to this, but I knew you wouldn't see me any other way." His eyes softened, his voice sincere.

Problem was, I'd fallen for his lying face too many times, and like the boy who'd cried wolf, I didn't believe him anymore.

He stepped closer, and all my nerves were shot. My muscles twitched, and a nauseating feeling overtook my stomach.

"I'm sorry I didn't tell you," I said, voice shaking. "I was scared, and I only wanted the best for Gracie."

"Gracie . . ." he whispered her name, as though he had just learned a new word and was committing it to memory. "Don't I get a decision on this?"

I nodded. "You do, and I'm sorry. It was a selfish decision on my part," I said, placing both hands on my chest. "But one that I thought was for the best. If you want to see her, if you want custody rights, we can come to a settlement. One where all parties are satisfied, but please . . ." I was rambling now, to the point of desperation. "Please don't drag this out in public. Let's not take this to court. She goes to preschool. She has friends, and we're friends with their parents. And Josh has a well-respected job. I just want to settle this quietly." My eyes, my voice, my being begged him to see reason.

His eyes grazed my face, his smile deepening. "You're still so beautiful, Sunshine."

I flinched. It was as if he hadn't heard a word I'd said. His sights were purely on me and me alone. If I didn't know better, I'd say he was using Gracie as a pawn.

When he reached for my hand, I jerked back. He wasn't allowed to touch me. I belonged to only one man, and that was Josh.

My hands pressed together. "Please, Hawke. I'm begging you, for Gracie's sake. Let's settle this out of court. We don't need money. We just want Gracie to be safe and happy."

"Fine," he said.

The air swooped out of my lungs, and my whole body relaxed at that one word. The one word that told me he agreed.

But then I watched him and waited for him to take it all back.

He held up a finger and stepped forward. "I want her life to be seamless, and you're right; as soon as the world knows that she's biologically mine, her life will never be the same. Paps will follow her everywhere. People will use her for the blood that runs through her veins. I don't want that to happen. Ever."

Sincerity was etched in his tone, and I wanted to believe him. I so did, but then his eyes turned expectant.

The hairs on the nape of my neck stood on end, the tension back in my shoulders.

"But I need something from you. You know I don't give anything without getting something in return." He smirked. "One kiss. That's all."

His words took me back to many years ago—our very first meeting when I'd been trying to get him to sign the postcard. Except, this time, I didn't feel attraction, only disgust and pity for the man in front of me. The once free-spirited young man had turned into an old junkie without purpose and without remorse.

I blinked, unmoving. I knew this decision would change the rest of my life, the rest of our lives.

What was one kiss in exchange for normalcy in Gracie's life?

One second, one move that could change everything.

"No." My voice was firm and resolute. I wasn't the same girl I'd been years ago. This time, I was taking a different route, making a better choice. "Love doesn't work that way. It's not tit for tat."

I turned to leave and ignored him as he called my name.

The next time he talked to us would be with our lawyer. I was done. Forever done with Hawke Calvin.

I waited.

We waited.

But his lawyers never contacted us.

And we never heard from him again.
I prayed that the heartbreak was over.
But it wasn't.

chapter SIXTEEN

Four Years Later . . .

"POWDER!" I RAN INTO THE kitchen, wondering where our new puppy was.

That dang dog and his inability to know that every corner was not his peeing ground. I swore, I needed to watch that little munchkin nonstop.

When Gracie had turned seven, she'd asked for a puppy, begged and pleaded and said she'd take care of it and do double duty on chores.

It had been months, and I still hadn't seen her pick up the slack.

Josh had shown up one day with a box that barked. We didn't have room for another living being in our two-bedroom apartment, but he had given me his puppy-dog face and sworn it was his life-long mission to make the girls in his life happy.

Josh and Gracie were working together on a Lego project on the coffee table while the TV blasted in front of them.

"Have you seen Powder?" My eyes perused the room.

Our two-bedroom apartment wasn't very big, yet I couldn't locate the little rascal.

"He's sleeping under your bed." Gracie's eyebrows pulled together into a straight line, an indication that she was in serious Lego mode.

"Why?" I propped my hands on my hips, huffing impatiently.

"Simple." Josh threw a smile my way. "He's scared of you."

I slapped one hand against my head. "Damn it. If he's in hiding, it's for a reason."

Four roses with their roots intact laid by Gracie's feet. I walked over, shook my head, and picked them up. Mud particles from the roots fell to the ground, dropping against the hardwood floor.

"Gracie, you can't keep taking Mrs. Timberstein's roses without asking her."

"Okay." She pushed out her lip in a pout, but her eyes didn't stray from the Lego castle in front of her. "I only wanted to get them for you."

I let out a soft sigh. Beautiful and smart, but also full of mischief. Gracie had a way of sweet-talking both Josh and me to get herself out of trouble.

"I'll put these in a vase." I walked to the kitchen sink. Taking out a pair of scissors from the drawer, I snipped the stems in a for-ty-five-degree angle, careful not to prick my hands on the thorns.

After filling the vase with water, I gathered the four beautiful long-stemmed red roses and pressed my nose against the velvet pet-als to take a whiff. "Thank you, Mrs. Timberstein." I smiled at my own joke.

Mrs. Timberstein owned the three-story apartment building next door. The front of her garden was filled with luscious roses in an array of colors. I always admired from afar, but Gracie wanted to admire the roses in a vase in our apartment

As I carried the vase into the living room, I felt the coldness of the glass against my palm. The scent of my vanilla candle infiltrated the air around me. And the sound of the television that everyone was ignoring played in the background.

Then, I heard four words that stopped my feet and my heart at the same time.

"Hawke Calvin is dead."

Everything that followed happened in slow motion, and the world around me became vividly clear.

From the corner of my eye, I saw Josh's eyes flip up to mine, but not before the vase full of water tumbled to the floor, the glass splintering into hundreds of pieces beneath me.

Josh shouted my name, his hand outstretched, knocking down the pink and purple Lego castle, but it was too late.

I had dropped to my knees on the ground.

Pain surrounded me, my legs, my head, my heart.

Josh screamed for Gracie to stay put while I glanced hazily at the screen.

It can't be true . . .

"Sam, you're bleeding!"

He reached for me, but I shook my head and stood.

"Stop, Sam! There's glass everywhere."

I walked toward the TV. A prickle of pain hit my right foot, but that was nothing compared to the searing ache radiating in the middle of my chest.

How could the beautiful newscaster with her long dark locks and her flawless olive skin be spitting out such hurtful words?

"Hawke Calvin, the lead singer of Def Deception, was found dead in his hotel room at eleven a.m. when his bodyguard went to check on him. Though it has yet to be confirmed, it is said that cocaine and heroin were found in his room, and an overdose is the expected cause of death. Hawke Calvin checked into rehab years ago but didn't finish the program . . ."

Pictures of Hawke played in front of me like a slideshow.

"Hawke rose to greatness as a teenager. His soulful voice and rugged edge led him to be discovered through YouTube. At the age of seventeen, he won his first Grammy . . ."

"Sam." Josh's presence loomed behind me, his voice oozing concern and sincerity and love. His hands flew to my shoulder. "Baby? I'm—"

I waved one hand in his direction. It felt wrong for him to comfort me when the man I was grieving had caused him the most grief in his life.

"Sam, you're bleeding."

"Mommy, are you okay?"

My eyes didn't move from the screen. I shook my head and uttered one word, "Please." My voice shook.

And because Josh was my soul mate and because he knew exactly what I needed, I heard him say, "Come on, Gracie, let's go to your room."

"But Mommy's—"

"Mommy will be okay," he said softly. "She just needs some time to herself right now."

He gently placed a washcloth by my hand and kissed the top of my head. That was when I peered up and met his eyes. He clenched his jaw, and it was as though he were going to say something, but he brushed the apple of my cheek with his thumb instead.

When they left, I took the washcloth and wiped up my knee and foot, noting the cut wasn't as serious as the blood around it suggested.

A chill ran through my body, and soreness spread through my lungs, making it difficult to breathe.

Tears blurred my vision as she repeated the words, "Hawke Calvin has died at the age of thirty-five."

And every time the words were said, the knife in my chest twisted.

It was as if repetition made it more real, the pain more intense.

I stared at the television, the sounds echoing from the newscaster's mouth leveled to a low buzz.

I had always wondered how people could be happily married one minute and, years later, be divorced and hate each other. Or how families who had grown up together could become estranged, never talking or speaking and only seeing each other at a funeral.

But, as I sat there, on my knees, bleeding, I understood. I realized you only hated someone so deeply because, at one time, you truly loved them. I hated Hawke because he'd hurt me, but my feelings, my love for him, had been real. Otherwise, the pain of his death wouldn't have filled me with such agonizing anguish.

And he loved me too just like my mother had loved me. They both loved me the best they knew how. But in the end their love for me couldn't trump their addictions and it wasn't enough to save their lives.

HAWKE'S FUNERAL WAS PRIVATE. I wondered who had gone, but I had not been invited, nor had I attended. He was laid to rest by his mother in Wisconsin, and later, I found out that was what he'd wanted.

The lawyer called me two weeks after his death—when it still hurt and it was still fresh and I was still crying. My days bled together, one day into the next.

I debated on not going, but I figured it had everything to do with Gracie, so I went by myself.

The heat of the summer sun directly beat down on me as I walked toward the same skyscraper I'd met him at before. But, before I stepped through the revolving doors, I froze. My hands shook at my sides, so much that I clasped them together to stop the tremors.

The last time I had seen Hawke, I'd been more than angry with him. I had said things that I wished I had never said and could take back. But, now, it was too late.

I blinked and squinted at the sun, praying that the tears would not escape, not now, not when I had to be strong.

I remembered what Josh had said.

"You can do this, baby. You loved him, and you want to honor his memory. Go see what they have to say."

I closed my eyes.

One breath.

Exhale.

And then I stepped through the revolving doors and entered the elevator bank, waiting for my destination—the same floor, the same office that I'd seen Hawke alive and well. When the elevator pinged open, I walked into the office and sat down in a waiting room after the secretary had taken down my name. When she led me down the hall and into a conference room, the two men in the room stood.

My eyes locked on a familiar face—Tilton. His red-rimmed eyes told me that the big guy was not without emotion.

Instantly, tears formed at the corners of my eyes. I charged toward him and hugged him. His facial features showed surprise right before he wrapped his arms around me. His stocky frame but gentle hands brought me to his chest, and my tears wet his polo shirt.

"You loved him, too," I whispered.

The shallowness in his breaths told me he was trying to keep it together. When he extracted me from his hold, the same lawyer I had met years back stepped forward.

"Mrs. Stanton, I'm John Bartlett. I'm sorry we have to meet again in such unforeseen circumstances."

I swallowed a lump in the back of my throat and swiped my tears with the back of my hand. I sat down next to Tilton. Our chairs faced Mr. Bartlett, the view of the city and Lake Michigan just beyond the floor-to-ceiling windows.

"I want you to know that I knew Mr. Calvin since he'd emancipated himself from his mother. He was more than just a client." His firm gray eyes met ours. "I was there through some of his biggest life changes. And I want you to know that Mr. Calvin's estate has been planned out for a very long time." He turned to face me. "Even before we knew about your child together."

My breathing slowed as I wrung my hands together on my lap.

What did he mean? Hawke had meant to leave me some piece of himself even before he knew about Gracie? Before she was even born and we were still together?

When I glanced at Tilton, his eyes were focused on the lawyer in front of us. I didn't have to wonder if he knew about Gracie because I was sure he did.

"What I will reveal shortly will come as a shock to you, but what isn't a shock is how much Hawke loved both of you. He cared deeply for you. As you know, he didn't have any family left other than the band members"—he nodded toward Tilton—"you"—then toward me—"and you, Mrs. Stanton."

I swiped at my eyes, unable to control my emotions. How heartbreaking to find out that, even after all these years, Hawke had still had very few close friends. Just hearing the lawyer state that Hawke had considered us his closest family put me over the edge.

"I'm just going to get through this." He cleared his throat. "Hawke Calvin's estate has been split between Tilton Mace, Grace Stanton, and you, Mrs. Samantha Stanton."

A gasp escaped me.

"This is a lot to take in." He pulled out six envelopes from his desk. "Hawke is currently worth one hundred twenty-three million dollars. This does not include the royalties that will continually pay out."

I cupped my mouth as my vision blurred with more tears.

I didn't want his money. I wanted him alive and well and in the flesh. I wanted things that would never happen. I wanted things money couldn't buy.

"He left each of you a letter and one for Grace to be opened when she's eighteen. In the other sealed envelopes are the trust agreements."

I wanted to cover my ears and not hear a word, pretend like this wasn't happening, pretend like he wasn't dead so that I could apologize over and over again for the last things I'd said to him.

"We'll need you to sign some paperwork, but I know this is a lot to handle for today." Mr. Bartlett stood and placed three envelopes in front of me on the desk, and then he handed Tilton his envelopes.

One gentle hand was placed on my shoulder as I cowered into myself.

"I'm sorry. Know that he loved you very much." Mr. Bartlett nodded toward Tilton one more time, giving him a sympathetic look, and then left.

All I could hear in my head were the words I'd last said to Hawke. All I could see was his face, full of regret, when I'd spit out my hateful words. All I could taste was the salt from my own tears.

"You're going to be okay." Tilton's jaw locked, as though he were using all his energy not to show any emotion, trying to stay steady. "You're going to be okay because that's what Hawke would want for you."

He extended one large palm, and I sucked back my tears. When I was ready, I blew out one shallow breath, picked up my envelopes, and placed my free hand in Tilton's.

We walked out, hand in hand, using each other for support. We were silent on the way down. I was sure thoughts of Hawke were raining in his head, as they were in mine.

When we exited the revolving doors, Tilton initiated one final hug. When he pulled back, his eyes were hopeful. "Can I see her?" There was a quiver in his voice, and I almost broke down again. "He says she looks just like him."

My face crumbled, and I nodded. "She does. She's beautiful," I whispered. "Of course you can see her."

Then, I watched as he walked away, his massive body almost comically huge as he strode down the busy sidewalk. My hands gripped the envelopes as I stepped into my car and locked myself in.

I stared in front of me, seeing nothing. I couldn't move. It was difficult to even concentrate on my next breath.

My shaky hands held the letter Hawke had left me, and I sat there for a long time.

Who knew how much time had passed?

When I'd exited the building, it had been daylight. Now, my stomach was grumbling as I took in the sun setting in front of me. I needed to do this before I went home to my husband and child. I needed to read this letter and put this behind me.

One breath.

One exhale.

Josh.

I needed to snap out of this sadness and be there for Josh.

It hurt to even move but I reached in my purse and texted my husband.

Don't worry. I'm just settling some stuff, and I'll be back home.

When I got home, that would be another bomb I would have to drop. We'd just become instant millionaires because of the death of someone Josh hadn't cared too much for.

My eyes focused on the white envelope. In the next second, I closed my eyes, and like Josh had taught me to do, I exhaled. Then, I opened the letter, and a sudden wave of emotion hit me, so hard that I clenched my jaw.

Seeing his handwriting, so signature to Hawke, reminded me of many years ago when all I had wanted was an autograph. My life and his life had been so carefree, and now, we were connected in a way that would bind us together for eternity.

     *

Sunshine, my only Sunshine,

I write when I get emotional, when I feel like things are getting to be too much to handle and I can't check out.

I saw you today with a little girl, and I knew she was mine before I even asked you. It's the most beautiful thing—to see my face fused with the most gorgeous woman I've ever met.

In another life, another time, I would have been the man for you. In our lives together, I wouldn't have been a rock star. I would have been a boy in love with a girl. Simple and sweet and so fucking beautiful. Just you and me against the world.

There were so many times I just wanted to stop. Run away from everything and take you with me. I should have. I wish I had.

I'm not mad at you, Sunshine. I know you did what you had to do, trying to protect our girl, and I get it.

In the darkness . . . through the pain, through the times when I was high as a kite, and I didn't know what was real . . . the one thing that I knew was real was you and me in Europe. In my bed. You in my arms. In my life.

You're probably wondering if I ever loved you. I said it so often, but I did things to hurt you. For that, I'm sorry. But, know this—I've never loved anyone more, Sunshine. You can question everything—why I acted the way I did, why I did the things I did—but know that I never loved any human being more than I loved you. You were my sunshine through the roar of chaos around me, through the pain that my mother caused me. You were constantly that voice in my head that told me to do better, and I'm so fucking sorry that I couldn't pull through this time.

Don't cry for me. In my short life, I've lived on overdrive. I've accomplished more than I ever thought I would. But the one accomplishment I made and one that will remain untainted forever is that little girl of ours. So, don't cry. I want you to live and teach our Gracie how to fly.

I know what you're thinking, but if you ever cared for me like I think you did, you'll let me do this. You'll take this money, and you'll do good with it. You'll take care of the only things that ever mattered to me—you and our child. You'll fulfill your dreams and your husband's, too, because I'm forever grateful for him. To do the things that I fell short on, to provide you with what I never could . . . to take care of our baby and raise her like she were his own, like she should be raised.

It's okay on this end. Wherever I am, I see light, not darkness. I feel calm, not pain. For once, I'm sure it's silent, but I revel in the silence where all I think about is you and our baby. Your light, your laugh, your love are all I see.

I love you for eternity, Samantha Clarke. And you will forever be my Sunshine.

chapter **SEVENTEEN**

GRAZING CATTLE, STUNTED TREES, AND endless yellow canola flowers outlined the road. As we drove farther down the country road, small farmhouses appeared. I stuck my head out the window, feeling the wind feather through my hair and the sun prickle my skin.

It had been months since I'd talked to the lawyer, and still, the fact that Hawke was dead had never sunk in. Maybe I was in denial, or maybe I wanted to believe it wasn't true.

The drive from Chicago to Wisconsin took four hours.

Hawke had been buried by his mother at Colossal Cemetery in Madison, Wisconsin. I hadn't been there at his actual burial, and I hadn't visited him. Every day though, I woke up with an ache in my stomach and a pain in my heart. And I knew I needed closure. I needed to let go of the way we'd left things the last time I saw him.

A deep breath escaped me when Josh pulled into the long winding road that led into the immense cemetery. The lawyer had given me specific directions on how to get to his gravesite though I didn't need to know. In the vast horizon, a stone angel stood. I knew it was his. Not by the description given to me by the lawyer, but the array of flowers lying on top of the headstone and at the angel's feet.

Josh halted the car and shifted into park. In that second, a cold sweat crept up my back, and a shiver ran through my body. I didn't know if I was ready for this, ready to see him, or ready to say goodbye. Seeing his gravesite would only confirm that he was truly gone and not roaming the world on tour.

Josh's voice broke through the silence. "Princess?" When I peered up at him, he reached for my hand, intertwining our fingers. One touch. His touch. "Do me a favor."

"Okay," I said, my eyes widening.

"Exhale."

And I did.

I blew out one long breath, exhaling all my hesitation away.

Then, he brought my hand to his lips. "Go. I'll wait for you right here."

I nodded, kissed his lips, and slipped out the door.

My purse hit my hip as I walked, the rustle of the wind blowing through my hair. The birds chirped in the background as I approached, and I took in the massive amount of roses and daisies and mums lying at the angel's feet.

Even in his death, Hawke was adored. Envelopes and papers were scattered along the edges of his tombstone.

Hawke Matthew Calvin
Life is a song. Sing it loud.

Heaviness initiated in my chest, and I sucked in a breath. My feet padded through the grass, inching toward the tombstone. I crouched down and then dropped to my knees.

My fingertips brushed against the marble. "Hey." Warmth formed behind my eyes, intense emotions bubbling to the surface. "I know you said you're not mad at me." I blew out another breath, trying to formulate my next words. "But I'm mad at myself." A single tear fell down my cheek. "I'm sorry for never telling you."

I blew out another breath.

"I'm sorry I said hateful things the last time I saw you." I swallowed.

I focused on his name etched on the gray marble.

"It's hard to believe you're not here anymore, not out and about, singing to your many adoring fans."

More tears. More sorrow.

"Tilton is hurting. We all are." I paused, not knowing what to say next.

Then, I decided to tell him all the good things. "I haven't touched the money yet. I didn't know what to do with it, how to honor your legacy, but Tilton is teaming up with a foundation called Cooking for Therapy."

When Tilton had approached me with the idea, I had jumped on board. Drugs had plagued my loved ones for as long as I could remember. And the idea of helping recovering addicts reverse the damage from their drug and alcohol use by cooking made it seem as though everything that had happened in my life would not be in vain. It had given me a new purpose.

"I just wish you could see it—Tilton's vision coming to life."

I sat Indian-style, running my fingers through the grass.

A few minutes of silence passed before I decided to talk about Gracie. "She's stunning, Hawke. Random strangers will come up to me and tell me she should model." I laughed. "And you know what? She knows it, too. She's cheeky and hardheaded but insanely talented . . . just like you."

I recalled their similarities. Too many to count, but he needed to hear them. "In certain light, when she's lying in her bed and she's sleeping, she's your twin. It's the dirty-blonde in her hair and in the greenest of green in her eyes that she's yours."

I clenched my jaw and pure emotion tore through me. The soreness in my chest heightened, spreading to my lungs, and more tears fell. "You know"—I swallowed—"she loves to sing. She has the most beautiful voice. It's angelic and powerful, just like her personality. She gets that from you because God knows Josh and I can't belt out a tune."

I paused, willing myself not to cry anymore. Too many tears had been shed.

"Thank you for her, Hawke. Thank you for this beautiful life you were able to give me. I know the circumstances were not ideal, but without you, without that night, there wouldn't be Gracie. And, for that, I'm forever grateful." My lips quivered with emotion. "I haven't opened the letter you gave her. I know she'll get it when she's eighteen, but before then, I'm going to tell her everything about you—when she's older and she can understand."

I started to choke on my own tears again. "I'm just so sorry . . . sorry that it took death to get us here, y'know? But she's going to know you, I promise."

I opened my purse, plucked out a picture of Gracie, and placed it on the tombstone. "I'll be back, and sometime in the future, I'll bring her." I kissed my hand and pressed it against his name.

Hawke Matthew Calvin

Life is a song. Sing it loud.

And Hawke had done that until his very end.

As I walked to the car, there was a lightness in my step. The ache in my chest was still present. I knew from experience that it would never truly go away, but I prayed it would dull eventually.

Josh was leaning against the passenger door, his ankles crossed. He'd been waiting for me all this time. When I approached, he held out a hand and pulled me into him, bringing me into the warmest embrace.

This was Josh. My Josh. The definition of love.

I basked in his embrace, and my whole body relaxed.

"You okay?" he whispered.

I nodded into his chest, squeezing him tighter. "Yeah." And I was.

Just like my mother's death, I knew it would take time to fully heal, but this had been a good step.

"I just want to go home and see Gracie."

He pulled back and smiled. "Then, let's go home, my beautiful girl." His words brought me back to many years ago when we had talked at the bar after his birthday. That time seemed like eons ago.

The drive back to Illinois flew by.

I had fallen asleep in the car, holding Josh's hand. When I awoke, the sun was beginning to set in front of us and I noticed we weren't taking our regular route to Chloe's.

"Where are we going? We're picking up Gracie at Chloe's place, right?"

"She's meeting us somewhere," he said vaguely.

I straightened in my seat to see houses on both sides of us, the orange of the light brightening the manicured landscape. We turned into a subdivision, and I quirked an eyebrow, studying Josh's stoic face. We were in our town but not in the vicinity of our apartment.

"Where is Chloe meeting us? At our apartment?"

"No. Somewhere else," he answered. Then, two dimples emerged on his cheeks.

This man and his sly ways. I swore, he was the king of surprises.

"Close your eyes," he said with a grin.

"What?" I did the opposite and only widened them.

"Why are you always asking questions?" he asked, both dimples popping on his cheeks. "Close your damn eyes, Princess. I'm trying to surprise you."

"Fine." Arms crossed over my chest but with a smile on my face, I did what I had been told.

When the car stopped, my foot jittered against the floor, and my hands wrung together in my lap. "You know I hate surprises."

"Liar! You just hate the anticipation of surprises." The door opened. "Sam, keep those eyes shut."

"They're shut! They're shut."

The warm breeze from the summer night hit my face as he opened my door. "Princess . . ." His voice softened with reverence, and just by his tone, I knew this gift—whatever it was—made him nervous. It was big.

He reached for my hand and pulled me to stand from the car.

"Can I open my eyes now?"

"Nope. Not yet." He flattened his hand against mine, feeling the inside of my palm. "What do you remember from the first time you saw me?"

I laughed. "Are we really having this conversation now?"

My heels dipped into the grass as he led me forward. "Yes, now. Tell me, what did you notice about me first?"

"Your smile."

I remembered that day so vividly. His dark chocolate eyes, the wave in his hair, and his boyish good looks. But Josh's smile was his signature—two dimples, pure happiness, no holding back. When he smiled, there was no way you couldn't.

"What do you remember about me?" I asked.

"Your hands," he said tenderly.

I shook my head, amused. "Yeah, I remember." The butterflies fluttered in the pit of my stomach as I recalled the memory. I lowered my voice into a manly Josh tone. "'You can tell a women's shoe size by the size of her hand.'"

"I remember everything about you that day," he said softly, turning my heart to mush. "Your hair was half up in a ponytail. You were wearing jeans and a bright aqua T-shirt with your Converse. When I saw you from across the room, I had to touch you to know you were real."

I sensed his smile through the darkness.

When I felt my hand getting tugged to the ground, I opened my eyes. His eyes twinkled against the sun setting in front of us. If I could snap a picture, it would look like a perfect proposal.

Josh knelt on the grass and right beside him was a shoebox. He opened the box, and in it were two glass slippers, one with a key.

"What's this?" I bit my thumbnail, practically hopping on both feet.

"The key to our house, from your Prince Charming."

His smile was blinding. The most beautiful thing I'd ever seen. He stood and placed the key in my hand, and then he framed my shoulders and turned me around.

My free hand flew to my lips as my eyes took in the quaint house in front of us. A ranch-style home that I had passed multiple times, admiring its character. The shutters were light gray, a pretty contrast to the white siding. A wide porch wrapped around the front, and rose bushes and lilies outlined the walkway.

I didn't get it. The house wasn't even on the market. I'd admired it for years from afar, but it wasn't available.

"It's ours," he said.

"How?"

He laughed. "I bought it."

"How?" I sounded like a broken record, but given that we'd been struggling to make ends meet, I didn't know how we could afford a house. It wasn't extravagant or massive by any means, but I'd thought it'd be a good five years before we could even think to buy one.

"I'm sorry." He gave me a guilty look. "I know we've been tight on money. It's only because I've been saving for this for a while."

I squeezed his hand tighter. "Don't ever apologize for taking care of your family."

He kissed me, and the touch of his lips was a delicious sensation. When my foot pressed against the first step on the porch, I held my breath, anticipation building inside me.

This was surreal—us, married and with a child, standing on our own front porch.

He pulled back and then nodded toward the door. "Go ahead."

I inhaled a deep breath and turned the knob. My eyes perused the inside of the house that was our new home, and my heart sang with joy—uninhibited, pure joy. There was a bounce in my step the further I went in. The yellow walls, the black and white tiles, the distressed kitchen cabinets, and the small fireplace could all be seen from where I stood. But what had my smile widening was the green-eyed beauty peeking out from the corner with her fairy god-mother, Chloe.

"Mom!" Gracie said before charging into my arms.

I bent down and crushed her into my chest. Warmth pooled behind my eyes as I showered her face with kisses. I'd missed my girl so much in the short time we'd been apart, and the emotion of the day was weighing me down.

"I love my room. I love this house," Gracie squeed.

"It's beautiful, isn't it?" I said, lightly touching her cheek.

Chloe leaned against the doorframe, a smirk on her face. "Congrats, homeowners. The least I can do is furnish my own room."

"Of course." My gaze was flooded with unshed tears.

Josh closed the gap between us, squeezing Gracie in the middle, like a human sandwich. His eyes held such reverence and such strength. "I know our lives didn't take the traditional route. First, baby, then marriage, and now, this. But"—he ducked in closer—"I wouldn't have wanted it any other way. Who knows if any other road would have led me to you?"

I gulped hard, swallowing back tears. This was my happy place—with Josh and Gracie.

And he was more than right. Our lives hadn't taken the traditional route. It had been a long and winding road, and there had been a couple of flats along the way, but here we were, together.

The people you loved, the people you spent your days with were the ones who mattered most. That was what made up a home. And for forever, until my last breath, Josh and Gracie would be my home.

"Thanks, baby. I love it." I kissed him through tear-filled eyes. "I love you."

And, now, it was time for my surprise.

"And I love us." I took his free hand and placed it on my belly, on top of the growing baby inside me—this time, half me and half

Josh.

His jaw dropped before he pulled back and assessed my face.

"Really?" he whispered, such hope in his eyes.

Because we'd been trying for years and because I'd taken three pregnancy tests to believe it, I nodded.

"Really!" His eyes dropped to my stomach and back to my face.

"Yes, baby," I confirmed.

He threw back his head and let out a loud whoop. Then, he bent down and showered my belly with kisses, then Gracie, and then me. "Thank you. I love you so much. Thank you. Thank you!" His joy was uncontainable, and both dimples were on display.

I cupped his face with one gentle hand. "No, baby, thank you."

Because I finally realized, fairy tales did come true.

And he was my real-life Prince Charming on earth and I'd forever be his Princess.

THE END.

Dear Readers,

Thank you for allowing this story to have a place on your bookshelf. I'm forever and ever grateful!

If you enjoyed this story, please sign up for my newsletter. My newsletter subscribers are the first to know about my upcoming releases and always have a chance to win an advanced copy of my book before it goes live.

Also, you just never know when some of these characters will stop by.

You can sign up at *www.authormiakayla.com*.

ABOUT THE AUTHOR

MIA KAYLA IS A NEW Adult and Contemporary Romance writer who lives in Illinois. She is the wife to the husband of the year and mommy to three unbelievable cute little girls who have multiplied her grey hairs.

In her free time she loves reading romance novels, jamming to boy bands, catching up on celebrity gossip and designing flowers for weddings.

Most of the time, she can be caught on the train with her nose in a book sporting a cheeky grin because the main characters finally get their happily-ever-after at the end.

She loves reading about happy endings but has more fun writing them.

HERE IS WHERE YOU CAN FIND MIA KAYLA:

JOIN HER READER GROUP:
www.facebook.com/groups/miakaylabooks

WEBPAGE:
www.authormiakayla.com

FACEBOOK:
www.facebook.com/authormiakayla

TWITTER:
www.twitter.com/authormiakayla

INSTAGRAM:
www.instagram.com/author_miakayla

GOODREADS:
www.goodreads.com/author/show/7382805.Mia_Kayla

ACKNOWLEDGEMENTS

TWO WORDS! I'M DONE.

There's an internal satisfaction after finishing a book that cannot be described. It's a feeling of great accomplishment. I remember the exact day that I finished this book. I called a writer friend and told her, "I'm done and I think I'm about to cry." And I was about to cry because it had taken me such a long time to get to that point. And obviously, when I said I was done, I was far from done because I still had to go through the editing and marketing and publishing process.

There were so many times that I doubted if I should even write this book, debated on changing some parts because I was afraid of reviews and worried about readers not liking it. But I had to stay true to the characters and the story line that was playing in my head so I trekked on.

This is a very different story than the other books that I have written. I usually write cheesy happy-go-lucky romance, but Samantha's journey is one with a lot more angst, more struggles and more heartbreak.

It took an army to get this done and to final form and I wouldn't have been able to do it without the help and encouragement of the following people.

First and foremost I want to thank God for that creative side of me that can't keep quiet and for the stories in my head that I have to share with the world.

To the real rockstar in my life—My husband. I love you because you support me in everything I do. And you watch the kids when I have to write.

To my writer friends that keep me accountable with daily word counts, keep me sane by listening to me vent and help me promote — To Michelle, Tracey, Danielle, El, Laura, Jaimie, Faith, Ryleigh,

Celeste and Kristy L. Only writers understand the struggles and insecurities of this journey and I appreciate each and every one of you. A lot of us started publishing around the same time and I'm so glad that we're able to grow in this path together. True loyal writer friends are hard to find.

To my family at Indie Chicks Rock, Alphas & Fairytales and Sassy Savvy— To Autumn, Molly, Kaylee, Allison, Willa, Jeanne, Dani, Sasha, Emery, Melanie and Claudia. Thanks for giving me a place to meet new readers, share my ARCs and party.

To my PA—Emily, you keep me organized and sane and happy. I'm so glad I met you. Thank you for all you do for me and our reader group. You are always keeping me on my toes and I appreciate you.

To my friend Jenn—Thanks for helping me from the very beginning. From organizing my sales to pimping my book, I know I can always count on you and your constant support of the Indie Chicks.

To my PR team from Sassy Savy Fabulous—Kristi, you are the bestest from the restest. Thank you so much for helping me market this book and pointing me in the right direction. Marketing is definitely not my strong suit so I appreciate your guidance and support.

To my rock star editing team — Oh my goodness, what would I do without you? Produce crap. That's what!

To my developmental editor, Megan— I heart you so much. So much! Thank you for helping me flesh out these characters and for always being honest with me even when the truth hurts.

To my copy editor, Jovana— You truly have an eagle's eye. Thank you for catching all my repetition and editing this book like it was your own. I'm the queen of repetition and I appreciate you keeping me in check.

To my proofreader, Shawna— Thank you so much for taking on a new client last minute. I'm confident after your last look that this manuscript is in tip-top shape.

To my formatter, Christine—You are the best in the business.

Thanks for beautifying my books with your graphics.

To my cover designer—Sommer, you've got talent and an eye for cover hotness. Thank you for putting your magic touch on my covers.

To my beta readers—Hot Tree, Amy, Alyssa, Emily, Lisa, Kaitie, Michelle and Sarah—I appreciate your feedback and also your friendship. Without you, this book wouldn't be what it is now.

To Kristy—Thanks for being my post beta reader and for loving this book as much as you do.

To Margie and my RRR Immersion partners—Thank you for Colorado and pushing me to become the best writer I can be. I continue to learn from each of you.

To the bloggers that have consistently supported me from my very first book to now. I heart you! Thank you for following me on this journey.

Last but not least to my readers— From those who have followed me from my very first book and to the new readers, thank you! thank you! thank you! I write for you.